SHADES

of SIN

SHADES
of SIN

Michele Vargo

TATE PUBLISHING & *Enterprises*

Published by Tate Publishing & Enterprises, LLC
127 E. Trade Center Terrace | Mustang, Oklahoma 73064 USA
1.888.361.9473 | www.tatepublishing.com

Tate Publishing is committed to excellence in the publishing industry. The company reflects the philosophy established by the founders, based on Psalm 68:11,
"The Lord gave the word and great was the company of those who published it."

Published in the United States of America

ISBN: 978-1-61663-300-4
1. Fiction, Family Life
2. Fiction, Christian, General
10.3.3

DEDICATION

This book is dedicated to my husband, David, who will always be the hero in my life story.

ACKNOWLEDGMENTS

Every writer is driven by the need to tell a story, but no one truly works alone.

My story was told not only with their technical help, but with the love and support of my children and a family who believed in me.

I would like to give special thanks to my early editors, Mark Hill and Carin Sutton, and the staff at Tate Publishing.

To Regan: I admire your work ethic and the way you follow your dreams. Your love and encouragement made me follow mine.

To David and Kimberly: You provided me with my first suitable text for submission. Thank you for your love and support.

To Robin, my hard taskmaster: Thank you for constantly reminding me that nothing is easy and for putting it all together and rescuing me. I couldn't have done it without you.

To Tim, my wonderful son-in-law who never says no.

And finally to David, who never lost faith. Thank you.

PROLOGUE

Sarah's reaction had shocked Claire, but now she felt only numbness. She had been wrong to come here. Sarah despised her.

She pulled her car alongside the road to let her breathing slow and with a trembling hand, turned the engine off. It was only now that she noticed her torn stockings and bleeding knees and gingerly leaned forward to pull a sliver of glass from her shin. Her palms were bleeding as well, and she reached across the seat for a box of tissues, wiping her hands first then the smudges they had left.

A wave of nausea swept over her, and she laid her forehead against the steering wheel. A light rain had started, and there was a chill in the air. The raindrops made tinny sounds atop the Buick.

But the creeping chill Claire felt had little to do with the weather. How had it come to this she wondered, hands shaking as they gripped the wheel. Without Sarah, there was no hope of redemption.

It was the end of everything she had hoped to accomplish. Claire allowed herself to calm and examined her cuts more closely. They were just superficial, a few glass slivers.

She finally felt some resolve of purpose. There was one more stop to make. She had to sit beside Jack—she had to make the belated apology—and only then could she fly home to David.

She would do things differently this time, though. No running out without making things right with Danni and Joe first. She would do her best to leave in a positive way. She owed them that much.

Claire restarted the Buick and turned toward the cemetery. It was almost over.

CLAIRE 2005

THE END OF EVERYTHING

How much sorrow can one heart hold? Claire wondered. She sat curled up on her chaise, shoulders slumped forward, heavy with the burden of guilt, composing letters that proved to be the most difficult thing she had ever done.

Her wastebaskets overflowed with rewrites. *How does one explain away four and a half years in a few words?* She sat deep in thought and finally came to the conclusion that saying less was a better option. Her final drafts were brief and unemotional. There would be time for emotions later. At least she hoped. And time for explanations and reasons.

It would all hinge on Sarah, of course. She would be the catalyst. If she could plead her case to Sarah and Sarah welcomed her back into the fold, the others would follow.

But for now, within these letters, there would be no excuses. She was going home—to explain, to seek forgiveness, to reconnect, to find peace. She was finally going home to find redemption … and to atone for her sins.

"Something to drink, ma'am?" Claire gazed right through the stewardess who leaned in toward her. "Would you like something to drink?"

She focused on the attractive stewardess and smiled. "Forgive me. My mind was elsewhere. Just some water would be fine."

The stewardess nodded and went about her business.

Claire's seatmate edged into her space. "I don't blame you for being distracted. I hate flying myself." He held out a hand. "Jim Connell, LC Electronics. I just know it's the end every time I board."

She squeezed his hand. "Claire Bradley."

"Oh. You're American. Going home?" he inquired.

"No."

"Business, then?" Claire merely shook her head and didn't offer more. Instead, she rummaged through a stack of magazines she'd brought for the flight. Mr. Jim Connell took the hint and didn't ask. When he picked up an airline magazine himself, she eased her head back and closed her eyes.

She wished the clock back. But, as Iris would say, "You can never go back. It's time to move ahead with your life, Claire."

The last few days had gone by in a blur. Once the thought entered her mind about going home, things had moved at

light speed. She'd just needed the encouragement—the push from Iris. She was as ready as she'd ever be.

How she wished Iris would have come with her. Their relationship, long evolved from doctor and patient to close friends, was, to Claire, a lifeline that had brought her back from the edge. She rubbed her wrists and the raised scars, finally fading after all these years. One year in the sanitarium, vaguely remembered; then two years of intense therapy with Iris and one year of readjusting to the real world.

She had a job now, in London. She worked at a charming bookstore within walking distance of her flat. She was in a new relationship. She was healing. But still she remained unsettled. Once she had made the decision to reunite with her family, all she needed was Iris's approval.

"I refuse to foster this relationship if it becomes a dependency, Claire," Iris scolded. "I like your company, but the psychotherapy is over and no longer necessary."

"David wants me to move in with him." Claire shrugged and smiled. "I just don't know if I'm ready for such a commitment."

Iris sighed. "He's crazy about you. Many young women would be envious of you." She stared out the window.

"When you left therapy, I told you that you could never become a whole person again until you confronted and reconciled your past, Claire."

Claire poured them each another glass of wine.

"Part of me wants to move forward with David, but part of me wants … no, needs to reconnect with my family.

I've made the decision. I'm going." She took Iris's hand. "Would you go with me?"

"No."

Claire gazed at the tiny flat that had become her refuge. There was nothing more to say.

She met David for dinner the following night at their favorite outdoor cafe. The air was damp and cool, and he wrapped his jacket around her shoulders when she caught a chill.

"I'll come with you. Really. I don't want you to do this alone."

Claire reached up and smoothed his unruly hair. "No." she smiled.

Some turbulence on the plane caused her to jolt in her seat. She sighed. Jim Connell of LC Electronics patted her hand. "We're okay," he reassured her. Claire lay back against the seat and closed her eyes once again. She'd been thinking of David, but now her thoughts turned to Jack and the path her life had taken.

CLAIRE 1969

THE BEGINNING

The first time Claire saw Jack Bradley was one month after her sixteenth birthday. She had just started her junior year at Montpelier High School and was working her first job at Benson's Ladies Wear downtown.

She was on a stepladder, hanging gauzy lingerie, when she turned and saw him standing there. He was in his army uniform, trim and erect and fine. He had a smile to light the room, and Claire was smitten. She blushed bright pink like the nightgown she was hanging.

"Excuse me, miss." Jack removed his cap. "I'm shopping for my girlfriend's birthday. I thought you might be able to help; you look about her size."

Claire's heart was thudding in her chest. She wasn't sure if she'd be able to speak. "What are you looking for?"

He smiled. "Well, what you're holding there looks pretty nice."

Claire turned around to place it on the rack. "You must be very close." She couldn't believe what she had said. *I'm an idiot*, she thought, biting her lip.

Jack threw his head back and laughed. He had a beautiful laugh. "I suppose we are." He touched her on her elbow, helping her down. Claire felt a thousand nerves tingling at his touch. "I don't suppose you would try that on for me?"

For a brief second, Claire almost said yes. She had never felt such feelings before. Some part of her wanted to show him. But he belonged to someone else. So instead she stood silent.

"I didn't think so," he said. "My name is Jack."

"I'm Claire." Claire wanted to shake his hand, to feel the electricity of his touch again, but Jack didn't offer.

"Anyway, I don't think she'd look nearly as pretty in that as you would be." Claire thought he could probably hear the pounding of her heart. Surely everyone in the store could hear.

"Are you in the army?" *Stupid, stupid, stupid!* "I mean, are you discharged or on leave or what?"

Jack couldn't seem to stop smiling. "Actually, I'm out. Did fourteen months in Vietnam."

Claire bit her lip. "I'm sorry for asking." Jack seemed hesitant what to do next.

"If you aren't the darnedest, prettiest thing I've seen since I've been home."

Claire felt faint. "What about slippers?"

Jack threw his head back, laughing. "I think slippers would be fine now." He grinned at her. "We'll save that pink nightgown for you."

Claire rang up some plain slippers, and Jack handed her the money, letting his hand linger on top of hers. She stopped breathing.

Jack leaned in close. "I would like to take you out," he whispered.

"What about your girlfriend?" Claire asked.

"We're not exclusive," Jack answered. "Besides, my interest has started to wane since I walked in here."

"I would like to go out with you." Claire breathed softly in and out.

"When?"

"I get off work Friday at seven."

"That's settled then. I'll be here at seven."

With that, Jack left the store. Claire could still smell his scent. She felt confused and strange. No boy had ever affected her in such a way.

Toby was a stock boy at the store and was in Claire's grade. "So those are the kind of guys you like." He sneered. "Baby killers."

Claire had never found the longhaired war protestors at her school attractive, and she bristled at his remark.

"You shouldn't say things like that. Besides, it's none of your business who I like."

"He's way too old for you; I know that." Toby went back to the storeroom.

Claire hadn't thought about his age, but Toby's remark was troubling. How would she explain to her parents that she might be dating someone older? Her father would never allow it. An introvert and a bookworm, Claire had never given her father a moment's cause for concern. At that instant, Claire made up her mind. She had to see Jack again. She would lie.

Before she left work that day, Claire did something amazing even to her. She bought that pink nightgown with her employee discount and decided she could go without lunch money that week.

Claire arrived at work Friday a few minutes before three. The anticipation of seeing Jack again had played havoc on her concentration at school.

She made up a story for her parents, telling them she had joined a study group for civics class that was required for senior year. Her father was impressed that his daughter was so conscientious about her studies and pleased that she had made some friends.

"We're getting pizza later, Papa," she called out at the door. "I'll be in by eleven."

Jack showed up ten minutes early and made her nervous while he watched her cash out. He looked amazing in his street clothes.

They walked side by side down the street to his car. Claire had never been inside a boy's car before. He saw her hesitate. "Would you rather just walk?"

"No, it's okay. Where are we going?"

"I thought we'd go park near the lake and talk; you know, get to know each other. Then we can go get a pizza or something."

Claire was apprehensive but excited, and when Jack grabbed her arm and scooted her close to him on the seat, she shuddered with delight.

Jack had a special place he parked, and when the car was off with darkness all around, Claire wondered if she had made a terrible mistake.

He pulled a couple of warm beers from the backseat and opened them with an opener hanging from the rear-view mirror beside a St. Christopher medal.

"You're Catholic, too?" asked Claire.

"Yep," he answered.

He slid his arm around her trembling shoulder. "Hey, baby, you cold?"

Claire shook her head.

"Well, you need to loosen up. Drink this beer straight down now. It'll warm you up all right."

Taking a swallow of beer, he asked, "So what year did you graduate?"

"A little while back," Claire lied. "What year did you graduate?"

"Nineteen sixty-three." He smiled at her. "And believe me, I'd remember you if you went to school around here." She shrugged and took a drink of beer. "Then a couple of years of JC before the draft. That's about it."

"Tell me about Vietnam."

"I don't like to talk about it much."

Immediately, Claire was sorry she'd brought it up. "It must have been hard."

Jack shrugged and encouraged her to drink up. He opened a second beer for her. "God, Claire; you're beautiful."

The beer made Claire feel soft and woozy. Jack kept stroking her arm and shoulder, talking softly about her hair, her eyes, her scent. His hand slid up her thigh, and Claire's breath caught in her throat.

"No," she croaked, barely able to speak. But Jack covered her mouth with his own, and his tongue probed inside, filling her with a delightful sensation. Claire moaned and halfheartedly pushed him away.

But Jack deftly laid her back against the seat and slid his fingers inside her panties.

"Oh, Claire," he whispered. "You're so ready, baby."

"No, Jack," she whispered. Claire's heart thudded in her chest at the shock of what was happening. She began to fight and paw against Jack, but his mouth continued to probe and his full weight was upon her in the tight space.

Her senses dulled from the alcohol, Claire wasn't sure what was happening, but the sudden pain and throbbing she felt below made her heart explode in her chest, and she knew it wasn't right.

Suddenly, it was all over. It ended as abruptly as it had started. She sat dazed, half-dressed in Jack's car, and sobbed.

"Jesus, Claire!" Jack stared at her incredulous, as if he had never even imagined such a thing. "You should have told me! I mean, at the store, the way you talked, I just thought... oh my God; I'm sorry your first time was like this."

Claire's face was buried in her hands. "I'm only sixteen." She sobbed.

Jack's face went white. "Christ, you're jailbait!" He zipped his trousers, opened the car door, and stepped out into the night. Claire slid her panties up and buttoned her blouse. She did her best to compose herself. Claire's mother had never spoken to her about sex, but Claire knew what had happened.

The car door opened, and Jack slid back behind the wheel. He stared hard at her anger touching his eyes.

"You should have told me. I never dreamed you were only sixteen the way you came onto me at the store. I'm twenty-four years old."

Claire whimpered. "You're mad at me."

He glared at her quivering frame pressed against the car seat and felt his anger softening. "Yeah. I am mad. I could go to jail."

"I'm sorry, Jack." Claire whimpered. "I wanted to be with you so bad.

"Oh, Claire." Jack shook his head. "You don't even know me. We don't know each other."

Claire clutched at him tightly. "Please don't leave me, Jack, please. I'll do anything," she cried.

Conflicted by his feelings, he reached over and pulled her into his arms. "This is crazy. This whole thing." The turmoil she created in him was new to Jack. This girl was different somehow. "Right now I'll admit it. I'm pretty crazy about you too, and I don't even know why." He shook his head. "I know that I shouldn't, but I want to see you again." He stroked her hair as she sniffed against his chest. "We'll work it out. Trust me."

They drove back to town in silence, his hand curled protectively around hers. They parked several blocks from Claire's house, and she did her best to make herself presentable. As she turned to leave, he pulled her around. He gripped Claire's shoulders and made her look at him. "You belong to me now; you need to understand that. I'll take care of things because you're my responsibility now, Claire. You're my girl."

Claire nodded. She belonged to Jack Bradley heart and soul.

Jack kept his word, and they continued to meet in secrecy. Claire lived for those few stolen moments with Jack.

SARAH 2005

THE LETTER

"Sarah, will you baptize my baby?" Sarah looked up from her patient's chart.

"What, Gretchen?"

"My baby, the one I'm taking care of, he's knocking on heaven's door. I mean, if you don't mind. The parents don't have anyone."

"Oh, sure, I'll be right there."

"We're over in the blue pod," Gretchen called over her shoulder as she hustled back to her patient. "Hurry!"

Sarah wondered how many babies she had baptized over the years. The younger RNs always came to her, no matter their faith; most found it a difficult task. She made sure that her own babies' alarms were on and that Beth would keep an eye and both ears on the pod; then she went to find Gretchen.

To Sarah, the baptismal rite was an obligation to each of the little souls they were unable to save. Gretchen's tiny patient was easy to find. The blue pod was crowded. Besides the young parents were some other family members, a crowd of Gretchen's coworkers bustling around the bed, the neo-doc, Dr. Azwar and the fellow, Felix Mczhez whom the nurses affectionately called "McCheese" and several onlookers. The crash cart was opened; the bedside was a mess.

Gretchen and her coworkers had done their best to provide a modicum of privacy by placing screens around the bedside, but it was minimal at best, and everyone in the room knew what was going on. The other parents couldn't help but stare and think, *I'm glad it's them and not us. Our baby is okay.*

Sarah knelt beside the young mom. "My name is Sarah. I'm here to baptize your baby, if that's what you want."

"Are you allowed to do that?" asked the dad. "I mean, are you authorized and everything?"

Sarah looked up at the young man. He had angry eyes—helpless, frustrated.

"Yes," Sarah replied thoughtfully. "I can officially baptize your son. You just have to give me his name."

"It's Brian. After me. Brian Scott Wilson."

"That's a nice, strong name—Brian." Sarah patted the mom's shoulder and rose to stand next to the isolette. The tiny infant was unresponsive. Only the ventilator vibrated away. He was a good size and gestationally looked to be about twenty-six or twenty-seven weeks. *A keeper*, Sarah thought to herself, trying to come to grips with the unfairness of life.

"Massive pulmonary hemorrhage," Gretchen whispered at her side.

Sarah closed her eyes and said a silent prayer. Then she opened a small bottle of sterile water, which she had just asked God to bless. "Heavenly Father," she spoke softly, "please accept this baby into your arms. Please grant him comfort and peace. As Jesus said, 'Suffer the little children unto me.'"

As Sarah poured water over the baby's forehead, she spoke. "I baptize thee, Brian Scott Wilson, in the name of the Father, the Son, and the Holy Ghost." Sarah made the sign of the cross on the tiny forehead with her finger. Then she stepped back and nodded to Gretchen.

Doctors Azwar and Mczhez, who had been standing alongside, nodded to the respiratory therapist, who turned off the ventilator. Gretchen had already silenced all the overhead alarms and worked quickly to undo all the cables, wires, and tubes holding the baby in the isolette.

When the noise of the ventilator ceased, the young mother sobbed and crumpled farther into the chair. Sarah laid a white baptismal cloth over the baby and helped Gretchen wrap him in a blanket to hand him to his parents.

After a few minutes, Gretchen and Dr. Mczhez checked the baby's heart rate with a small ultrasonic device called a doplar. They shook their heads. "Time of death: three-oh-six."

Gretchen's coworkers put their arms around the sobbing mother and helped walk the family to the bereavement room. "We'll bring Brian to you."

They brought the grieving family coffee and pitchers of water, a phone, and boxes of tissues. Someone paged

the social worker on call. The family would have to decide on a funeral home and arrangements.

Gretchen began removing the remaining lead wires and catheters from the small body. He would need to be bathed and dressed. Sarah stopped her for a moment, physically turned her around, and hugged her. Gretchen stifled a sob and wiped tears from her eyes before she pushed Sarah away. "Stop that," she complained. "I'll never get this baby to his mother."

Sarah pitched in to help. The RNs were always the last to cry, often taking their tears home. Sarah understood loss and pain well. She identified with all her coworkers whenever they lost a patient.

She felt she could identify with the parents as well because she had suffered death and loss, but never—thank God—a child.

Gretchen shooed her back to her own patients. "There're enough people in here to help. Beth probably needs a break. Get back to your own pod. Thank you, Sarah."

Sarah stopped by the nurses' station and filled out the information for the baptismal certificate. Being able to offer such a comfort as baptism to parents who had lost a baby was one of the reasons Sarah loved working at St. Anne's. She loved the diversity and commitment from the staff to provide equal care for all people. She felt they were a family and took pride that it didn't matter whether the parents were rich or poor. Each of their tiny patients received the same quality care, and every nurse gave the best he or she had to give.

By morning, she was dog-tired. *I'm getting too old to work this shift*, she thought. The sky was lightening, and

the hospital was awakening with the sounds of morning activity.

After report, the nurses gathered around the time clock, laughing and joking with one another. Everyone had a hug for Gretchen. Tonight, Gretchen would be given an "easy" assignment so that she could recoup emotionally. They all tried to protect one another.

Drew was a young nurse who had been with them for about four years. "Hey, Sarah," he called, "we're going to the Nightcap for a drink. Why don't you come along? Even McCheese is coming."

Dr. Felix Mczhez was doing a fellowship in neonatal medicine after doing two rotations during his residency. He was a "smart" resident, meaning he recognized early on that he was green and unskilled and that he could learn a lot from nurses with years of experience and expertise.

The staff nurses liked and respected him. They had a great deal of difficulty dealing with his name, and whenever he pronounced his name for them it came out sounding like McCheese. Felix good-naturedly accepted his nickname.

"Thanks, Drew. I'd love to come, but I have to get the girls off to school."

Sarah hoped to catch some good sleep today. Abbie's soccer game was at four o'clock, and Aimee would be home at three thirty. The benefit of the graveyard shift was being home in the morning to get them off to school and home when they got off the bus.

Matt had been watching for her car to drive in and hustled out the front door.

"I've got a full day, and I want to leave early for Abbie's game." He leaned in and pecked her on the cheek. "How was your night?"

Sarah shrugged. "Okay. Kind of rough. Gretchen lost her patient."

Matt squeezed her shoulders. "I'm sorry, babe. Get some sleep, okay?"

"Are the girls ready?"

Matt looked sheepish. "I did my best."

"Hmm." Sarah furrowed her brow. "I know what that means."

"Got to run." Matt slid into his car and drove off. She dragged her tired body into the house. The girls were at the table with their cereal bowls.

"Mama! Mama!" they cried.

Sarah delivered hugs and kisses to each one. "You're not dressed!" she scolded.

"Daddy wanted us to wear dumb stuff!" Abbie cried in defense.

Abbie, almost nine, already had her own sense of style; in fact, she had insisted on picking out her own clothes since she was four. Getting dressed often led to arguments, and Aimee was already picking up bad habits from her older sister.

Sarah always rued the mornings when she and the girls hadn't decided on a particular outfit the night before. Uniforms weren't required for the elementary students, but Abbie would start wearing them in middle school. Sarah couldn't wait.

Thus, they were almost late for the bus when Sarah ushered them out the door.

She watched from the porch and waved at the bus as it drove away. Heaving a sigh, she shooed Brutus in the house and trudged upstairs, where she gratefully climbed into her pajamas and warm bed. She could smell Matt's scent on his pillow and curled around it. Brutus curled onto the rug next to the bed.

"Didn't you just get up?" Sarah asked him. The dog yawned. "Unbelievable," she said before she closed her eyes.

The doorbell was persistent, ringing and ringing until Sarah opened her eyes. "This can't be happening." She moaned. She squinted at the clock through her burning eyes. Eleven thirty. Brutus was sprawled on the bedside rug. "Don't you hear that? You don't even bother to bark? What kind of a watchdog are you?" The dog lazily lifted his head then lolled over to the other side. "I should have named you Tinkerbell."

Wrapping a heavy robe around her, she went downstairs and peeked through the window to see the mailman, Harold. That's why Brutus hadn't barked. "Unbelievable," she whispered to herself.

Sarah opened the door a little.

"I'm sorry. I knew you'd be sleeping, but I have a registered letter for you that you need to sign."

"Unbelievable," Sarah repeated. She opened the door all the way. "Where do I sign?"

"Right here." He gestured while Sarah scratched her name; then, tipping his hat, he bounded down the steps.

"Maybe I won a sweepstakes," she called after him.

Sarah rubbed her tired eyes and yawned. The letter was from England. Sarah stared at the envelope for a time before sitting down on the sofa.

England—the letter was from her mother. She ran her fingers over the address. She would have recognized her mother's writing anywhere. She'd waited so long for this, and now she just stared.

Finally, she sighed, stood up, and walked to the secretary in the den, where she pulled the grainy photo from the drawer. Her mother, arm in arm with a young man, smiling and loaded down with bags, was leaving a department store. The photo had arrived with a report from the private detective who had found her. He had reported that her mother was "doing well" living and working in London. *Doing well*, Sarah thought bitterly. *While we were mourning her, she was doing well.*

Sarah tore open the envelope and removed a one-page letter. After reading it, she sat down and called Matt's office.

"Cofield Dental; may I help you?"

"Karen, it's Sarah. Can he talk, or is he with a patient?"

"Well," Karen's friendly voice answered, "his mouth is crammed full of jellyrolls. Dr. Cofield brought in a box this morning, and the both of them are back in the lounge scarfing down donuts." She chuckled. "Hold on. I'll put him on."

"Sarah," Henry Cofield warmly greeted her. "What are you doing up? Matthew said you had rough night."

"Well, maybe I heard the two of you were eating donuts instead of doing your work. Now what kind of example are you setting as dentists, hmm?"

Henry chuckled. "You caught us red-handed, dear. I plead guilty as charged. Now you can lecture that husband of yours."

Henry passed the phone to Matt. "Say, what's up? Everything okay?"

"Is this what you meant by a 'full-day'?"

Matt laughed then suddenly realized that Sarah wasn't laughing.

"Matt, I got a letter from my mom. She's coming home. She wants to know if we'll see her, if someone will pick her up at the airport next week, which is a lot of nerve, if you ask me. She sent a registered letter here. And it says she sent one to Danni."

There was silence now from Matt's end.

"Matt, are you there?"

"Yeah, I'm here. Just…surprised. But I guess that's good, right?"

Sarah paused. "That's good?"

Matt read the change in her tone.

"Sarah, I know you're exhausted. It's not even noon. We've got a week to talk about this. There's no need for you to get upset right now. What you need is sleep. Don't you have to go in tonight? Sarah?"

"What."

"I know you're upset. I'm not blowing you off or anything. Just don't get shaken up now. Please. Just go to bed, and we'll talk about it at Abbie's game, okay?"

"Sure." Sarah rang off. "Unbelievable." How could Matt even think she could go back to sleep now? She had to think. She stood in a steamy shower and let the hot water flow over her shoulders. She was filled with angry tension.

How can this be happening? she wondered. *No contact for years, and now suddenly she's coming home. Just when everyone was healing.*

Sarah dressed in warm sweats and pulled her hair back in a pony. She called Danni and got her answering machine. "Call me," was the simple message she left. It didn't take her long to make it out of the house. She grabbed her keys and cell and drove toward her parents' home.

It had been at least a year since she had been to the house. Matt took care of things. He paid a landscape company to keep the yard immaculate, a cleaning company three times a year, and a neighbor to keep a check on the house. He also paid the utilities and the taxes, and Rob kept the inside in good repair.

Rob could fix anything. Dad had been so against Danni marrying him, and yet Rob had proved himself to be worth his weight in gold. Anytime Dad had needed a handyman, Rob had been the guy he called.

Sarah parked in the drive and unlocked the front door. She laid her cell phone beside her mother's old one on the hall tree. Her footsteps echoed on the hardwood, and Sarah couldn't help but think back to the last time she had stood in this foyer with her mother.

SARAH 2001

THE MEMORY

Sarah knew what was best for her mom. She and Matt had discussed it on a daily basis since Dad's funeral. If Mom would just agree to come stay with them, even if just for a while, she'd have the girls to take her mind off Dad and Sarah could keep her busy. She certainly hadn't been herself. Sarah had rehearsed over in her mind how to broach the subject, but Danni's objections kept encroaching on her thoughts. The last thing she needed now was to fight with her sister.

Danni had argued with her. "Why should Mom live with you? I'm the one having a new baby. She was planning on coming to stay with me when the baby came anyway."

"Don't be ridiculous, Danni," Sarah had countered. "Of course she'll stay with you a few weeks after the baby

comes. I'm talking about long term here. You and Rob certainly aren't set up to keep Mom on a long-term basis. Matt and I have the space to put her up and give her enough room to maintain a little independence."

Danni slouched down in her seat a little, a classic Danni pout. "I don't want our house to be gone forever."

"That house is just too much for mom to keep up, and it's filled with pieces of Dad. Besides, she doesn't have to give up the house right away anyway. The house could be rented out for a year or two until Mom gets back to herself."

Sarah pulled up at the house, clearing her mind of everything else. She had to find the right words to convince Mom what was best for her. Sarah had always been good at winning arguments, and she squared her shoulders on the walk to the door of the home she had grown up in.

Her reaction when she saw the two bags all packed by the door was confusion. For one moment, Sarah was dumbfounded.

"Mom?" She stood staring at the suitcases, all her carefully chosen words escaping her. "Mom? Where are you off to?"

Claire walked into the foyer, drying her hands on a dishcloth. She looked resolute. "I'm going away, Sarah."

A little unsure of herself, and suddenly realizing that she was going to have to change her words, Sarah walked past her mom into the kitchen. "Let's have coffee and talk, Mom."

Claire stood, dishcloth in hand, picking at her nails. "I don't have a lot of time. I called because I'm going away and I needed to tell you."

"Mom, that's why I'm here. I agree wholeheartedly. Matt and I talked, and we both feel you need to get away too. That's why I came as soon as you called, to bring you home with us."

Claire looked incredulous. Sarah wanted to reach out and touch her mother, but something stopped her. She sat down gingerly on the kitchen chair. Claire leaned against the wall.

"I didn't say I was getting away, Sarah. I said I was going away. I'm leaving for Europe."

Now Sarah was incredulous.

"Europe? Where in Europe?"

"I'd rather not say. I just am not sure where I'll end up, and I need to be alone."

"You'd rather not say?" Sarah's voice was almost a whisper. "Look, Mom. If you want to see Europe, we'll work things out. Matt has vacation time coming, and we'll look into Europe. We're pretty open, and the girls would love it."

"You need to listen, Sarah. You've always had a difficult time hearing me. I'm leaving. Alone. I'm not a wife anymore, and I…" Claire hesitated and lowered her head. "I can't do this mother thing anymore. I'm sorry."

Sarah felt as if she'd been struck in the stomach. "What do you mean by that?" Her heart pounded suddenly. "You don't want to be a mother anymore?"

"I can't be a mother anymore. I just… can't. I can't do"—she gestured around her—"any of this."

Now anger flooded over Sarah. "So when things get tough, I should just abandon the girls? Are you just going to abandon them, Mom? What am I supposed to tell Abbie? And what about Danni? 'Oh, sorry, Danni, Mom would have loved being here for the baby's birth, but she just couldn't be a mom anymore.' Does that sound right? Huh, Mom?"

Claire's shoulders slumped. "Say what you want. Say whatever you need to say. I can't stay here. I can't be sorry anymore. Just tell them whatever you want, Sarah. I don't care. Just tell them I'm gone."

"I don't believe this; I mean—you can't be serious, Mother. I realize that you're depressed. I understand what a loss you're feeling. We all feel Dad's loss. But talking crazy like this...I refuse to believe that you would hurt Danni and Joe and the girls by taking off right now. We've all just gone through one loss, and now you want to put everyone through even more."

"My cab should be here in a few minutes."

"A cab? Why a cab, Mom. Why am I not taking you to the airport if you're really leaving?"

"I don't want anyone to know where I'm going. It's for the best."

"The best." Sarah felt as though she'd had the wind knocked out of her. She hadn't seen this coming. Not at all. She couldn't let her mom just leave. She couldn't.

"When are you planning on coming back?"

Claire averted Sarah's eyes. "I'm not coming back. I want to be alone."

A horn sounded in the drive. Claire picked up both her suitcases.

Sarah was close on her heels. "What about the house, Mom? I need to know how to get ahold of you. What if something happens to Danni? Please, Mom, don't do this."

But Sarah's pleadings fell upon deaf ears. Claire was speed walking to the cab. Sarah followed. Her mother didn't respond or turn. The cab pulled out of the drive. Sarah thought of jumping into the car and following the cab, but she was angry and didn't want to give her mother the satisfaction.

Instead, she walked back into the house. The house keys were laid on the hall tree, along with her mother's cell phone. The cat mewed from the kitchen.

"The cat!" She spoke out loud, arms wrapped around herself. *What am I supposed to do with the cat?*

SARAH 2005

A HOUSE OF SECRETS

Clementine had come home with Sarah and Matt and had not thrived, but rather, had survived Brutus and the girls. They had grown accustomed to one another, and after the novelty wore off, the girls finally stopped tormenting old Clementine. Sarah honestly believed having Grandma's cat had helped Abbie through the rough times.

Aimee, at two and a half, had adjusted much easier than Abbie, then four. Abbie and Claire had what Sarah thought was a special bond. She shook her head. How wrong she had been. At least on her mother's part. Explaining to a four-year-old that her grandmother no longer wanted to be a part of her life had been the most difficult thing Sarah had ever had to do. Hiding her tears, anger, and grief from her girls had been equally hard.

Sarah walked into her dad's den and stood with her arms folded across her chest. His address book was still on top of the desk. Sarah thumbed through it briefly, seeing names from the past.

She took the stairs to her parents' room. Most of the furniture was covered. Joe had stayed at the house three summers between semesters when he worked for Matt at the dental office, but since graduation and the new job in Chicago, the house stood empty.

She opened her mother's bureau drawers. Sarah felt uneasy violating her mother's drawers. She looked at the closet and the boxes of photos on the top shelf. Looking around, Sarah pulled the vanity stool over and hauled two heavy boxes down. They were filled with family photos. Some were very old.

Mom and Dad's wedding photo. How young she looked, like a child. Abbie's face. A red blotch was noticeable on her cheek. Sarah touched the photo. Mom looked like a deer caught in the headlights. It was definitely Abbie's face, only a bit older. She put the photograph aside.

Dad's honorable discharge papers were in the box. Mom had provided the papers, and the legion had presented her with a flag for his coffin. Some time after Mom left, Matt found the flag in a box in Dad's den and gave it to Joe.

Sarah dug farther into the box. There were photos of the three of them growing up. Some nice pictures of Mom and Dad in each other's arms, Mom looking up at Dad, smiling as if he were some kind of superhero.

In the second box, Sarah found their baby books. Sarah's was the most complete. She'd done the same thing with her own girls, writing down everything for Abbie and more lax when it came to Aimee. Joe's book was almost empty—only the first few pages filled out.

Sarah found her birth certificate. Mom's age was listed as sixteen; Dad's age twenty-four. She stared at the record. *That can't be right. Mom and Dad met at Northwestern.* Her diploma was right on the wall downstairs next to Dad's. Mom was twenty-two when she was born. Sarah stared at her mother's wedding photo. She looked sixteen.

Sarah's head was spinning. Sixteen! How could that be? That would mean that her mom was now fifty-two. And she thought her mother was fifty-eight. No wonder she looked so young in that London photo.

Sarah found a cigar box in the bottom of the box. It contained a photograph of what Sarah believed was her grandparents. Mom had said that all of their pictures had been destroyed in the fire that took their lives. Her grandfather looked tall and stern. Her grandmother looked young. She was beautiful, with dark glossy hair and eyes like Mom and Abbie. Sarah and Aimee had inherited their ashy blonde locks from Dad.

Sarah compared it to her parents' wedding photo. They were in the same dress. She was almost sure of it. But there was more material around the waist in her mother's photo. Sarah stared at the pictures, a horrific thought scratching at her psyche. *My mother was pregnant. My mother was sixteen and pregnant!*

Sarah found their marriage license in the cigar box. Claire Abigail St. Germaine. Age sixteen. Jack Marlon Bradley. Age twenty-four. Quickly, Sarah put everything back in its place and stowed the boxes back on the shelf, leaving the room as it was.

She ran back downstairs and took her mother's diploma off the wall. It was dated 1970. Sarah was born in 1969. And her dad's was dated 1969. Sarah was angry with herself for not having this compulsion before now. Why hadn't she questioned things before this? Mom had always been closed to questions about her grandma and grandpa. About how she and Dad met and dated. About her college days.

She rummaged through the drawers in Dad's desk until she found a phone book. No listings for Northwestern locally. She picked up her cell and called directory assistance.

It took over an hour for Sarah to find out the answers she sought. Her mother never graduated from Northwestern. But the bigger shock was that her father hadn't either.

Sarah curled up in her dad's chair. Their whole life had been a lie. She tapped the cell phone against her knee. Should she call Matt? Danni? Where was Danni? Why hadn't she called?

Sarah wondered how much more heartbreak Danni could handle. The doorbell chimed. Sarah rose and peeked out the side window. It was Mrs. Bloom, the neighbor.

"Mrs. Bloom." Sarah smiled warmly.

"Is everything okay, Sarah? I saw your car pull in, and I was just concerned that something was wrong."

"No, nothing wrong. I came by to check on some things. But since you're here, I wonder if I could pick your brain a little about my parents."

"Of course, I'll tell you whatever I can, Sarah."

"I'd offer you some coffee, but we haven't been using the house for a year and cleaned out all the foodstuffs."

"Why don't you come next door with me? I've got coffee brewing and a fresh batch of cookies from the oven. Mr. Bloom is at the gym. He still does his workout, you know."

"That sounds wonderful," Sarah said as she followed her out the door, keys in hand, locking it behind her.

It had been years since Sarah had been in the Blooms' house, and nothing had changed. It was like stepping back into the seventies. The cookies smelled wonderful, and Sarah was grateful to curl her hands around a steaming cup of coffee.

"What can I help you with, dear?"

Sarah pulled her mother's folded letter out of her sweatshirt pocket and showed it to Mrs. Bloom.

"Oh, heavens." She looked shocked. "Has it been four years?"

"Yes." Sarah nodded. "Four and a half, actually."

"Oh, Sarah. How difficult this must be for you." Mrs. Bloom patted her arm.

Sarah sighed heavily. "I'm just trying to deal"—she shrugged—"with the letter; her coming home after all this time. It's such a shock. We were all just healing as a family, and now this."

Mrs. Bloom said nothing, just squeezed her hand tightly.

"We never sat down and talked after the funeral and after Mom left," Sarah said. "I guess now I want some things answered. I'm just trying to make sense of it all. If there was something I did—or anyone for that matter—that would make her run away."

"No, no." Mrs. Bloom clucked her tongue.

"Your mother was very troubled, Sarah. She was so young and fragile. A child herself. She so loved your father. Idolized him. But he was like a father to her in so many ways."

"So my mother was not twenty-two when I was born."

Mrs. Bloom looked into her eyes. She hesitated.

"It's okay," Sarah reassured her. "I found their marriage license and my birth certificate. They both state my mother's age as sixteen."

"Your mother was a very private person. But she was an only child. And Jack was an only child. "When your grandparents died in that house fire, I just remember how heartbroken she was that your grandmother never got a chance to see you. Your mother had just convinced Jack to make the trip to her parents' home when the fire killed them. I think she believed she had reconciled things with them when the fire occurred. The fire marshal classified it as an accidental fire, even though he told your dad that it was arson."

"Arson!"

"That fire was deliberately set. Your mother told me she suspected her father set the fire that killed them both so that he would never have to lay eyes on you. The police detective called it a murder-suicide, but the fire marshal was a friend of your grandfather, and he would have nothing of that because of the church."

Mrs. Bloom saw the shock and anguish on Sarah's face. "I'm sorry, dear." She shook her head. "I don't mean to be so insensitive."

"No," Sarah stated firmly. "I asked you. I need to know."

Mrs. Bloom sipped her coffee. "Well, there was no one for your mom to talk with. Jack's mother was already

dead when they got married, and his dad lived in Florida. There was just no one else for your mom. So she often came to me. She was quite pregnant when she married. And only had been on one date with your father. She said it was her fault. She led him to believe that she was older. He was just out of the army when they met. She lied to her parents and went out with him. Sex on the first date, and her a virgin, no less. She said she really didn't understand how it happened."

"Date rape," Sarah said.

"No, Sarah." Mrs. Bloom pointed her finger at her. "Your father was an honorable young man. He went to your grandfather and asked for your mother's hand. Your grandfather threw him out of the house."

"How did they end up getting married, then?"

"Well, your grandmother intervened. Claire said she didn't know what her mother said to him, but the next day, she started making arrangements at the church and took down her wedding dress from the attic. Your grandmother was altering the dress when your grandfather walked into the room, and when he saw your mother's swollen belly. he knew. His face said it all. Your grandfather was from the old country, and it was still a stigma back then for a good Catholic girl to become pregnant before marriage. Mrs. Bloom sighed and patted Sarah's hand. "More coffee, dear?" She stood up and filled Sarah's cup before she could answer. Then she sat back and looked at Sarah's stricken face. "Do you want me to continue?"

"Yes."

Your mother sat at this very table and told me that the day of the wedding, your grandfather stopped in the anteroom where Claire was waiting and said awful things

to her. He said she was no better than a common street whore and that she shamed her mother's fine white wedding gown. And she said he was so enraged at the sight of her he slapped her face so hard that it knocked her over. Then he told her that the only reason he had agreed to walk her down the aisle was to prevent her mother from being ashamed and ostracized. He swore that he would stay for the ceremony but that he would never lay eyes upon the bastard child she carried."

Tears sprang from Sarah's eyes. Mrs. Bloom jumped up and grabbed a tissue box. "I'm sorry, dear."

Sarah shrugged her shoulders. "What a wedding day." She sniffed.

"Your mother said she walked down the aisle that day with your grandfather's handprint on her cheek."

"That explains the wedding photo." Sarah chewed her thumbnail.

"Well, after that they moved here, and your dad's work started taking off better after they lived here a few years.

Sarah changed the subject. "The other thing is their degrees from Northwestern."

"Oh, those." Mrs. Bloom chuckled. "Your father purchased those. They're phonies, of course. He said it helped him get ahead at work, and back then, no one ever checked on those things much."

"Why does my mother have one?"

"Well, she said that your father insisted. Said he'd be embarrassed for people to know that his wife wasn't even a high school graduate. That's why they started telling people she was a lot older than she actually was."

Sarah finished her coffee. "Thank you," she said patting the old woman's hand reassuringly, even though she was starting to feel uncomfortable. "I really appreciate it."

"I can't imagine how hard all of this is for you, my dear." She shook her head.

"My goodness; look at the time! I thought Mr. Bloom would be home by now!"

Sarah glanced behind her at the wall clock. Four fifteen. Her face registered shock. Panic swam over her. "It can't be four fifteen."

"Yes, dear, that clock is right."

"Dear God, I have to run. Aimee gets off the bus at three thirty."

THE MISTAKE

Sarah sprinted across the yard and remembered her cell phone on the hall tree. She had missed two calls from Matt. She dashed out of the house, jumped in her vehicle, and sped out of the subdivision, redialing Matt's cell.

"Hey! Where are you two? I didn't remember if I told you the game was clear over at St. Pius'."

Sarah interrupted. "I went to the house and lost track of time. I'm headed home now."

There was a pause.

"Where is Aimee?"

"I'm headed home now." Sarah's voice was shaky. "I told you, I lost track of time."

"Aimee's home alone?"

"I'll be there in five minutes."

"Is the dog out?"

"No. I left early. He's in the house."

"There's no one around that neighborhood during

the day, Sarah. And Aimee's home alone; locked outside!" The fear and anger in Matt's voice was unmistakable.

"I know that, Matt. That's why I'm hurrying. I'll call you back." Sarah clicked the phone off and tossed it in the seat.

She turned the corner of their house and felt nausea creeping up her gut—no sign of Aimee. Sarah pulled in, braked, and jumped out of the car.

"Aimee!" she cried out. Sarah's heart pounded as she ran frantically up the steps of the porch, looking in the corner. "Aimee!" Panic caused her voice to crack. "Aimee!"

She ran toward the back yard, her heart hammering.

Aimee had heard her mother's anguished cries, but she was frightened and angry and chose to ignore her.

Sarah rounded the corner of the house.

Then she caught sight of her out back on the swings, wisps of blond hair poking out from her hat, her bright pink backpack on the ground.

Sarah ran to her. Aimee's face was tear streaked. She had been crying so hard that her breaths were making little hiccupping sounds.

Sarah fell down on her knees, cradling her in her arms. "Oh, baby. I'm sorry."

"You left me all alone." Aimee wouldn't look at her.

"You're okay, baby." Sarah spoke soothingly, petting her head. "You did the right thing. You stayed home and went to the backyard. You're a good girl, Aimee."

Sarah stood and tried to pick her up, but Aimee stiffened.

"It's okay. We have to call your daddy and let him know that you're all right."

Sarah forcibly picked her up off the ground. She was so small and light. Sarah's own heart was still pounding in her chest. She wiped at Aimee's tears as they walked, her little face red and swollen. At the car, she grabbed her cell phone and dialed Matt's number.

"She's okay. I've got her. We'll come to the game."

"Don't bother." Matt couldn't disguise the anger in his voice. "The game will be over before you get here."

Sarah hesitated. "I'm sorry, Matt."

"Me too. We'll be home later." Matt clicked off. Sarah stared at the phone in her hand.

"Come on, baby; we'll go in and get your school clothes off."

Sarah took time helping Aimee off with her school clothes, even though she was quite capable of dressing herself. She needed to touch her, baby her, redeem herself. Aimee still avoided looking at her with those hurt eyes.

Sarah helped her into some comfy sweats. "Do you have papers to show me?"

"Why weren't you home?"

Sarah cupped the little face in her hands and covered it with kisses. "Aimee, I'm sorry. I didn't mean to be late. I went to Grandma's old house and lost track of the time. I'm mad at myself."

"You're supposed to be home for me."

"Yes. You're absolutely right. I did the wrong thing. Sometimes moms make mistakes. Look at me. Look."

"Moms aren't supposed to do the wrong thing."

Sarah put a finger on her chin again. "I promise you it won't ever happen again. Do you understand that, Aimee? I'll be here. Okay?"

"Okay."

Sarah and Aimee were seated at the kitchen table when Matt and Abbie got home. Abbie had been crying too. Her face was clouded and angry. Matt walked directly to Aimee and picked her up. He folded her into his arms.

Sarah reached out to hug Abbie, who pulled away. "I'm sorry I missed your game."

"I scored a goal, and you weren't there to see it."

Sarah pulled Abbie into her arms and squeezed her tight. "I'm really sorry, Abs. I really am sorry."

"I'm hungry."

"Why don't you girls grab a cookie and go upstairs for a few minutes while I talk to Mom. Take your backpacks too."

The girls grabbed their backpacks and a cookie and headed upstairs.

Matt waited until the girls were out of earshot and turned on Sarah. "You just couldn't leave it alone, could you?"

"Look, Matt, I said I was sorry. I just lost track of time. I know you're mad because I missed Abbie's game."

"I'm mad because you forgot a six-year-old!" he screamed at her. "Anything could have happened to her. There's no one in this neighborhood! What if some pervert would have been driving by?"

"She's okay, Matt. Nothing happened."

"This time." He countered, "We're going to work on a contingency plan with the girls for when there's no one home."

"Don't you dare say that to them." Sarah's voice shook. "I already told Aimee—I *promised* her that it wouldn't happen again."

"What were you doing at your mom's house?"

Sarah sat down. She wished she could take back the entire day. "I don't know. I just felt I had to go. I'm sorry. I really screwed up."

"Don't you work tonight?"

"Yes."

"So you've had no sleep today and you're going to work tonight. Well, I don't think I'd want you taking care of my baby."

"Don't be an ass," Sarah whispered.

"I'm going to pick up some pizzas or burgers or something." Matt picked up his keys. "You might as well lie down for a while." The door clicked shut behind him.

Sarah sat at the table, hugging her knees. *Thanks again, Mom*, she thought. *You've succeeded in screwing up my life once more.* Sarah felt drained. She climbed the stairs and walked to the girls' room. They were coloring.

"Dad's bringing home pizzas or burgers." They ignored her. "I'm going to lie down for a few minutes. I'll leave my door open in case you need me."

Sarah lay back on her bed and sighed. She had no intention of sleeping, but suddenly Matt was shaking her.

"It's nine thirty," he said.

Sarah woke disoriented. The room was dark.

"I thought you'd want time to shower."

"Are the girls still up?"

"No. I told you it's nine thirty. They had a bath and ate. There's some cold pizza. Get a shower, and you can nuke it."

She sat on the edge of the bed and tried to get her bearings. "I didn't realize I would sleep so long."

Matt walked downstairs without another word, and Sarah went in to shower.

Everything came back. The steaming hot water revived Sarah somewhat. She dressed in clean scrubs and ponytailed her hair. With minimal makeup on, she made her way downstairs after checking on the girls and kissing them good-bye.

Matt was in the kitchen putting a couple slices of pizza on a plate. "You've got to feel like hell."

"Not so bad physically." Sarah shrugged. "My mental condition sucks."

"You gonna show me the letter from your mom?"

Sarah reached into her sweatshirt pocket and handed the letter to Matt. He read it slowly then looked up. "Danni's already called about four times. She's a little shook up."

"Oh God." Sarah groaned. "Did she call Joe yet?"

"No, but I talked with him and told him."

"Matt."

"Were you going to hide it from your brother, Sarah?"

"I suppose you think we should just all be happy to hear from her. Please don't tell me you think we should reconcile with her." Sarah sat down and chewed on some pizza Matt put in front of her.

"I think you should reconcile with your mother. I think you need to at least try."

"Unbelievable." Sarah dropped her pizza. "One day with my mother back in the picture, and my life is in turmoil."

"You created the problems today, Sarah, not your mother."

"Thanks for that, Matt."

He shrugged. "What do you want me to say?"

"I said I was sorry. More than once. I made a mistake."

Matt's eyes were hurt. She could read the disappointment in them. "Anything could have happened to her. Anything."

"You're absolutely right." Sarah pushed the pizza away. "But thank God, nothing did. So can we just get past it?"

Matt didn't move. Sarah sighed and pushed her chair back. "Well, I'm going to brush my teeth and go."

She stopped once more in the girls' room and kissed them good-bye. She and Matt had often discussed separate bedrooms for the girls, but they protested. As much as they argued and bickered, they were close and still needed to share space.

Matt was waiting by the door with her keys in hand when she went downstairs.

"I'm going to worry about you driving after not getting any sleep."

"Don't. I'll be fine."

"Okay." He touched her arm. "I'm over it."

They stood awkwardly outside Sarah's minivan.

"I'm sorry I acted like a jerk," Matt said.

"I'm really sorry too. It was a dumb mistake."

They kissed and hugged for a long time. "I'm going to be late." She pushed him back.

Sarah drove without the radio on, enjoying the silence in the car. Matt's scent surrounded her from her clothes. How right the world was when she was in his arms.

SARAH AND MATTHEW 2005

TIES THAT BIND

On the drive to work, Sarah allowed her mind to drift back to the first time she met Matt Law. She was still on orientation in the NICU.

Sarah's patient was born with two front teeth. Matt, doing a pedodontic residency, came on consult and promptly pulled the two teeth, much to the amazement of the student nurses, most of whom Matt flirted with as they gathered around to watch. He was tall with dark hair, huge hands, and a cute smile.

He wasn't the kind of guy women would say was handsome; they would describe him as a "real" guy. As Sarah would later tell her friends, "He's the kind of guy that cleans up really well, as long as I'm there to tell him

not to wear corduroy pants and tennis shoes at the same time."

That day, Sarah found herself jealous that Matt was ignoring her. *It's my patient*, she thought.

"Doesn't it hurt?" she asked out loud.

Matt grinned. "No. The teeth really aren't rooted,"—he leaned toward her badge—"Sarah."

After he left, all the students talked about how cute and single he was.

"Hmmph," Sarah added. "He wasn't that cute. I thought he was full of himself."

Their paths crossed in the cafeteria later that day.

"Hey, Sarah."

Sarah stopped, tray in hand. "Hi."

Sarah's friends stopped with her, but Matt stared only at Sarah. "Will you eat down here?" He gestured toward the cafeteria tables.

They talked through lunch. It came easy. And Sarah kept thinking, *What a decent guy. He just seems so nice.*

They started dating, and soon Sarah took Matt home to meet her dad. Matt handled Jack great, realizing he had to "win over" the dad in order to win the daughter. His knack for talking to people charmed Claire.

Then Matt took Sarah to meet his parents. Matt's parents were polite and aloof. They felt strongly that their obligation was done, and although they would always keep in touch and wished them well, warmer places were calling them.

They stayed around for the wedding (which Sarah thought was perfect) then headed south. And even when the girls were born, there were pictures and cards and let-ters exchanged, but they were little more than polite correspondence, and they continued to show little interest in their son or his family.

Sarah felt that the first years of her marriage were the best of her life. Matt fit into her family circle as if he had always been there.

The memories of those good times made Sarah feel melancholy. So many wasted years since her dad died. And the thought of the family dealing with another heartbreak was too much to bear.

By the time she reached the parking deck and found a spot, Sarah had to sprint to the time clock without a minute to spare.

She wasn't the only one, and her friends laughed and wrestled to get to the time clock first. The locker room was alive with chatter, friends exchanging pictures of their kids, updating one another about their lives. Sarah loved her job.

No matter how tired she was, arriving at work energized her.

The unit was abuzz with activity. Tonya Kennedy was in charge on second shift and was huddled over the assignments. She would distribute the patient load according to acuity, needs, and nurse experience.

Tonya would need to consider admission rotation, off-unit procedures, discharge teaching, and who would cover C-sections and deliveries.

"We've had five admissions since morning," she explained. "Staffing is tight. Two of them are one-to-ones." She bent over the paper and rubbed her temples.

"Sarah, I gave you the worst kid, a bad PPHN." She looked up apologetically. "You look tired; are you up to it?"

Sarah patted Tonya's shoulder. "Sure. A busy night is what I need to keep awake. Besides, I'm sure everybody will help."

"Don't count on it," Gretchen teased.

SARAH'S NIGHT

Persistent Pulmonary Hypertension of the newborn was a difficult disease process to manage and carried a high mortality rate. With new advances and technology in neonatology such as nitrous oxide therapy, outcomes were improving. Sarah would be taking report from Kenyatta Howard, an African American RN who had been her preceptor in orientation. Kenyatta often seemed intimidating to parents because she was tall, opinionated, and loud. She was also a fierce patient advocate.

Sarah thought her actions were expressive and beautiful. And she loved the way Kenyatta defended her tiny charges.

She met Sarah at the door to the isolation room, hands on hips.

"I told them not to give this baby to anyone but you because you know how to manage this case. I know you know this because I taught you."

"I do," Sarah responded.

Kenyatta stood aside. "Well, come in, then. My body's tired, and this baby needs a guardian.

"I ordered McCheese to bed," she continued. "This poor baby has been bothered far too much tonight."

Sarah began taking notes while Kenyatta talked.

"Baby boy Kolgen. First name, Ethan. Parents are William and Heather. He's a fertility baby, and they been trying a long time. I put them both up in the overnight room. Told the dad that Mom needs some rest; she's all done in. Reassured him we'll come for them if his condition worsens."

Sarah nodded.

Report took a long time, and Sarah took notes, nodding from time to time. There was a lot of information to cover, and Kenyatta always gave a thorough report.

You have an x-ray at six a.m. He needs a weight, but do not attempt to weigh this baby by yourself. Get at least one other person. He's paralyzed. I know what a hot shot you are at intubation, but Azwar would not be happy."

Sarah nodded. "Right."

Tonya showed up at the door. "Sarah, you have a call. It's your sister. I told her you were in report and I'd have you call back, but she says it's urgent."

Sarah bit her lip. "Excuse me, Kenyatta." She picked up the phone.

"Danni."

Kenyatta found herself privy to half a conversation.

"I can't talk now...I realize it's important...Danni, I'm not blowing you off. I have a critical patient. I'm in the middle of report...Danni, I can't tomorrow. I need to sleep. But can we do Wednesday? Breakfast? Well, what about lunch, then? Braccio's? Okay, eleven o'clock...Danni, I know you're upset. Just hang on, and we'll talk it out. I love you, too. Bye."

Sarah hung up and sighed. "I'm sorry."

"Sounds like I didn't do you any favor signing you up for this kid."

Kenyatta was one of the few people who knew about Sarah's mom. "She sent a registered letter to me and Danni. She's coming home. Danni's freaking."

"I'm sorry, Sarah. You've got to be stressed out yourself."

"I just wish she'd stay away."

"She probably needs to make amends."

"Well, she won't be making amends with me," Sarah snapped. "I hate her."

"Sarah! You do not mean that." Kenyatta pointed a finger at her. "She hurt you deep. But you need to examine that hardened heart and find some forgiveness there. Living with all that anger and hate isn't good."

"I won't ever forgive her, Kenyatta," Sarah answered defiantly.

Kenyatta shook her head.

"Then you'll become a bitter old woman. A mother's love is a powerful thing. You have daughters. I would think you would know that."

"I would never abandon them."

"When your girls are grown and gone, you don't know what things will be like. And she didn't abandon you if she's coming home. She just took herself a sabbatical. A long one. I could use one myself."

Sarah couldn't help but smile.

"You fool." She chuckled softly. "Are you ever going to finish report? I'm not gonna stand here and gab all night. I have work to do."

"Hmmph. Where was I? Drips." Kenyatta scanned the cardex.

She went over all the IV drips, medications, and labs. "Oh, yes. You'll need to draw a midnight CBC and gas. You might want to add a bili and calcium." She yawned. "That's about it, I guess. All the history. Last thing is the parents. You know, they're scared white kids, Sarah. They've just been given a lot of information that they weren't ready for. They'll need help and a lot of reinforcement."

"I get it." Sarah smiled and took a breath. She was going to have a very busy night ahead. "I'm sorry I held you up. Thanks for listening. Now go home."

Kenyatta patted her hand. "I'll be back in the morning."

"In the morning?" Sarah asked. "After a double shift today?"

"I have to see this through. I wouldn't be able to stay away thinking about him." Kenyatta waved as she walked away.

Sarah shook her head. Gretchen and Debbie popped in. "What do you need?"

"Coffee. And I'm gonna need some help weighing later. But right now, I'm gonna sit down and figure out how I can coordinate tasks as much as possible so I'm not disturbing this little guy."

Even with help from her coworkers, Sarah was busy the entire shift. Her midnight blood gas was better than she expected, and when she called McCheese, he was hesitant about what to do.

"Felix, I really think that less is more in this case. We need to decrease this baby's stress. Besides, we have other issues. I noticed some irregular beats and PACs on the monitor, so I added a potassium and calcium level to the bili."

"Good move. Okay, Sarah. We'll follow your lead. But I do want you to hold the bicarb drip for now. Maybe the kid is really going to respond to the nitrous. And call me with those labs."

"Will do. Thanks, Felix."

Sarah ended up giving two calcium boluses and changing her hyperal to add more potassium and calcium. Drew and Gretchen helped her weigh Ethan at about five a.m. and did a "snatch and grab" with the soiled bed linens and placed fresh blankets in the isolette.

The antiquated tube system was out of order, and Debbie and Colleen made countless trips back and forth to the lab and pharmacy.

Sarah was huddled over the covered bed with the lights dimmed, working through portholes, when she turned and saw the young man leaning on the doorjamb.

"William?" she inquired. He nodded. "I'm Sarah. I'm taking care of Ethan this shift."

"Kenyatta told us. She said you were the best nurse here."

Sarah smiled. "Actually, the best nurse here is the one who left earlier. Kenyatta was my teacher."

The young dad shook his head. "You know, we've waited so long. Thought everything was okay. This is so hard on Heather. If anything happens to Ethan..." He bit his lip, choked back tears. "Well, I don't know how Heather could handle it."

Sarah closed up the bed and took William by the hand. "I have about twenty minutes before Ethan has an x-ray. Let's go sit down and have coffee."

Drew sat outside the door to cover while Sarah led William to the family waiting room.

They sat at a rickety table and drank bitter-tasting coffee in foam cups. Sarah said a silent prayer to find the right words.

"William, did the neo docs talk with you?"

"Yes. You know"—he shrugged—"they were busy with the baby. He said we'd talk more on rounds today. But I guess we just don't understand the condition or how to explain things to our family."

"Well," Sarah began, "it isn't easy to understand or explain. PPHN stands for persistent pulmonary hypertension of the newborn. A long name, I know. The condition is difficult to treat and has a high mortality rate because of all the associated complications. It's very frustrating for caregivers.

"It's also difficult to explain. You see, the pathways that normally happen for a newborn to breathe outside the womb didn't quite happen for Ethan. There was a glitch. Remember how dusky he looked?"

"Yes."

"Well, there's a problem with vascular resistance causing an abnormal blood flow pattern that we call 'shunting.' Everything we're doing is to try to get that vascular smooth muscle to relax. The ventilator is giving him low tidal volumes at high frequencies.

"It's like rescue breathing. We need to keep him sedated and quiet so the ventilator can do the work. We're supporting all his body systems. I'm not going to say he's improving, but he's holding his own."

"Will he survive?"

Sarah took William's hand. "I honestly don't know. There has been a great deal of success with nitrous oxide therapy."

A tear escaped and ran down the young father's cheek. He didn't seem to notice.

"Do you and Heather belong to a church?"

"Yes. Our minister is coming up today."

"Good. Prayers are always welcomed. You can also have Ethan baptized."

He stared at Sarah. "Do you think we should?"

"I'm just saying you can, William. Ethan is still considered critical."

"Are you a person of faith, Sarah?"

"Yes."

"Why do you think God would do such a thing to Heather and Ethan?"

"I don't know." Sarah looked away. "None of us understand God's plan, William.

"But I do believe that you will find the strength. Use your faith, William. Your faith will see you both through this. You and Heather will find the strength."

William stood up. "I'm keeping you from Ethan."

"Yes. I should get back. But whenever you need to talk, we are all in this together."

"Thank you, Sarah."

Sarah hugged the young man. "Sometimes we forget that dads need hugs too."

They walked quickly back to the unit.

"Heather wants to visit, but I don't know."

"Sometimes they get strength from their parents. Just having a familiar hand laid on them. It might comfort them both. A mother's love is powerful, William. Sometimes it can move mountains."

"Okay."

Sarah hustled back to the isolation room and thanked Drew. The x-ray tech showed up with the portable machine at 6:10 a.m., and after that, Sarah drew morning labs.

Before she knew it, Kenyatta was standing in the doorway and it was time to give report. Kenyatta was pleased with the numbers.

"Dad might bring Mom in for a visit. You know," Sarah said, "a mother's love can be a powerful thing."

Kenyatta smiled. "It's good to know that sometimes you listen with one of those ears."

Report took thirty minutes, and most everyone was gone when Sarah clocked out at 7:40 a.m.

The drive home was long, and she was almost too tired to push down the gas pedal. Matt was waiting in the drive when she arrived home, coffee cup in hand.

"I was starting to get worried."

Sarah shrugged her shoulders. "I'm okay."

He wrapped his big arm around her shoulders and walked her in. The girls were scrubbed clean, dressed, and sitting at attention at the table.

"Hi, Mom," said Aimee.

"Hi, babies." Sarah yawned.

"I'm gonna stay and get the girls off. You go to bed," Matt ordered.

For once, Sarah didn't argue; she passed kisses all around and trudged up the stairs, Matt and Brutus in tow.

"Are you gonna be all right for this afternoon?" he asked her hesitantly.

Sarah stifled a yawn, pulled her scrubs off, and donned her pajamas. "I'll be okay. I'm going to set my alarm."

Matt waited while Sarah brushed her teeth and washed her face, and then he tucked her in.

Sleep came easily, and she didn't even hear Brutus when he curled up on the rug next to the bed. Her sleep was dreamless and undisturbed.

SURPRISES

Sarah slept straight through until three p.m. then jumped up, put on coffee, and was waiting on the porch in her pajamas when Aimee got off the bus.

Aimee's face was excited and relieved. Sarah hugged her and helped her off with her backpack. Aimee, normally her quiet child, was animated and chatty.

"There's a field trip to the children's museum, and you can go," she told Sarah as she rummaged through her backpack. "I have a note!"

"Cool," said Sarah. Aimee found the permission slip and handed it to Sarah.

"Can you go?"

"Well, let me see the date and time," said Sarah as she read. "I think so. Won't it be fun?"

Aimee looked pleased. "I'm hungry."

"How about some cookies and milk while I have my coffee?"

Abbie got off the bus soon after. Unlike Aimee, Abbie seemed glum. "Have a bad day?"

Abbie shrugged. "No."

"Are you still mad at me for missing your game?" Abbie didn't answer. "I'm sorry, Abs." Sarah settled her at the table with Aimee then went upstairs to shower. It wasn't long after that Abbie walked in the bedroom and plopped herself on the bed.

"Get up, please; I was just going to make that," Sarah chided.

"Why? You'll just be going to bed soon."

"Because that's what civilized people do." Sarah pointed to the door. "I think you should start your homework if you want to have some TV or telephone time after dinner."

"Dad said Grandma is coming home."

Sarah stopped, turned. "That doesn't mean we're going to see her."

"I want to see her!" Abbie shouted, stamping her foot.

"Don't raise your voice to me, young lady!" Sarah scolded. "It isn't up to you to decide."

"It's not fair. I want to see Grandma."

"I'm not going to argue with you, Abbie. You're eight years old, and Dad and I will do what's best for you."

"I'm almost nine!"

Abbie had never been her age. She was "almost five" when she was four, "almost six" when she was five, and now she was "almost nine."

"Abbie, I don't even know if Grandma will want to see you; she's been gone for years and may just be coming home to settle some of her affairs."

Abbie's face looked stricken. Sarah regretted her words immediately.

"She'll want to see me." Abbie jutted her chin out.

Sarah sighed and sat down on the bed. "I don't want to see you and Aimee hurt again."

"Even if she doesn't stay, I want to see her. Please, Mom. I want to see Grandma."

"We'll see. I'll talk to Dad. Go do your homework. Please, Abbie. I don't want to fight tonight." Sarah approached her daughter and wrapped her arms around her. She was growing so fast. Such a beautiful girl. Dark hair and eyes, long legs like a colt. *So much like Mom in looks, with my personality*, she thought. Stubborn, willful, confident. Aimee looked more like Sarah with her ashy blonde hair, but there was no mistaking the similarities between her own personality and Abbie's.

"I'll do my homework, but I still want to see Grandma. I'll give up TV and the phone for a week if you want," Abbie said on her way out the door.

Sarah suddenly was exhausted. She was angry with Matt for discussing the letter with Abbie. She finished dressing and made the bed. Her curling iron was hot, but her plans to fix her hair were dashed, so she ponied it and applied minimal makeup.

She made her way downstairs after checking on the girls, who were on their bedroom floor, Abbie doing her homework and Aimee coloring.

"I'm going to start supper!" she hollered on her way downstairs.

Sarah knew she needed to calm down. The last thing she wanted to do was fight with Matt tonight. Knowing Abbie, she probably had been full of questions about

where she and Aimee were and why her dad was so upset. Sarah knew that Abbie could be formidable.

She started chicken enchiladas, the girls' favorite dinner, and pulled a bag of rice down from the shelf.

The phone rang. It was Matt. "I wanted to make sure everything was okay."

"Everything's fine." Sarah started to say something but held back. "Are you going to be home on time?"

"That depends. Is there a beautiful woman in the kitchen cooking dinner?"

"Aren't you the lucky one?"

"I should be rolling in by seven. Do you need me to pick anything up?"

"Hmm ... it's Mexican night for the girls. How about some chips and salsa?"

"You got it. See you soon. I love you."

"Love you too."

Sarah busied herself around. Maybe they could get the girls off to bed early and have a good talk about mom.

The girls moseyed down soon after. "Homework done?"

"Yes."

"Well, why don't you girls set the table?"

"What's for dinner?"

"Enchiladas and rice."

"Cool!"

"Is Dad going to be home?"

"Yes."

The girls unpacked the dishwasher and set the table.

Abbie opened the back door for Brutus, and immediately he was circling around Sarah's feet, whining for dinner.

"Abbie, feed the animals please before Brutus chews off one of my feet!"

"Why do I have to do everything?" Abbie whined. "Why doesn't Aimee have to do anything?"

Sarah was exasperated. "Abbie, can you just do what you're told without whining for once?"

Abbie stamped her foot. "It's not fair!"

"Abigail Claire, if I hear that phrase once more from you, you'll go to your room before your dad gets home!"

Abbie quit whining and fed the dog and cat. There was no way she wanted to miss her dad. Aimee stood in the kitchen doorway, smiling. Abbie stuck her tongue out at her sister.

"Aimee, you can get that smirk off your face and carry those folded clothes upstairs and put them away."

Aimee frowned. "Yuck!"

Abbie smiled.

Matt came in a few minutes before seven. Matt folded the girls in his big arms and smothered them with kisses. Then he wrapped his arms around Sarah's waist.

"Go entertain the girls; the enchiladas are too hot," she said as she pushed him away. But he wouldn't let go until he nuzzled her neck and yanked her ponytail holder out.

"Matt, quit!" she scolded. "Stop!"

He laughed, chased both girls around the table, snapping at them with the ponytail holder, and ran into the living room. Both girls and the dog pranced after him.

"Tackle!" she heard him holler. "Loss of yardage!"

The girls squealed and giggled. Brutus barked.

"No football in the living room!" Sarah cried to deaf ears.

The enchiladas came out of the oven perfectly golden brown and bubbling.

"Come and eat!" she called to the crew. "Not you, Brutus."

Sarah didn't know how they were done with dinner by seven thirty, with the girls chattering throughout the entire meal, but everyone pushed their plates back and had eaten well.

"That was great." Matt smiled.

"It's late. Let's get moving, guys." Matt scraped and rinsed their plates and loaded the dishwasher while the girls cleared the table and Sarah put food away and cleaned the stove and counter.]

Then they all gathered their laundry together and put a load in. At 8:10, the girls went upstairs and got into their pajamas and brushed their teeth.

Choosing an appropriate school outfit only took ten minutes; the girls sensed that their mother was in no mood for arguments.

"You have a half hour to watch the Disney Channel," Sarah called.

"A half-hour!" Abbie complained.

"It's past eight thirty!" Sarah shouted. "No arguments."

"What about a snack?" cried Aimee.

"A snack? Aimee, we just got up from the dinner table!"

"Ice cream bars!" cried Matt from the kitchen.

"Yeah!" chimed the girls.

Sarah groaned with exasperation.

After seeing the girls off to bed, Sarah climbed into her own pajamas and brushed her teeth then settled on the sofa with Matt, who was zoned in on the TV.

"Hey, can we talk?" she asked.

Matt turned off the TV.

"I'm thinking we should get the girls pagers or cell phones."

"Awesome!" came Abbie's voice from the stairs.

"Abbie!" Matt yelled. "You're supposed to be in bed."

"I know," she said. "But if you guys are going to talk about Grandma, I want to see her. I really want to see her."

Sarah stood up tall and faced her daughter with clenched jaw. "Go to bed now, Abigail." She hissed. "This is not for you to decide."

"Why, Mom? Why don't you want us to see Grandma? Just because you don't love her anymore? Well, I love Grandma, and I want to see her!"

Sarah walked up a step, her arm pointed toward the bedroom. "Go now."

Abbie spun around, her face stricken with tears. "I wish you would go away!"

Sarah's shoulders slumped, and she shook her head. Matt took her by the hand and pulled her into the kitchen. He poured them both a glass of milk.

"She's just a little kid, Sarah. She didn't mean it."

"I know, but it hurts just the same. I don't understand why she wants to see her so bad, I mean, after what she did."

Matt shrugged. "Children have a great capacity for forgiveness. More than we have. Abbie just remembers the good times with Grandma."

Sarah was filled with sadness whenever she remembered the good times with her mom. "Well, I don't want to see her."

"I think the girls are old enough to decide for themselves if they want to see your mom."

"Fine," Sarah snapped. "We disagree."

"You need to ask yourself if you're protecting them or trying to punish your mom."

"I am trying"—"she clenched her fists—"to protect them from heartbreak. Again."

"Oh, Sarah. Everyone experiences heartbreak in life. It's how you survive that heartbreak, what you walk away with, that defines the kind of person you are. The girls are capable of making that decision for themselves."

Sarah sat quiet, thinking.

"I talked with Joe. We're going to pick your mom up at the airport on Friday and take her to the house."

Sarah couldn't believe what she was hearing. "You're unbelievable."

"I knew you would be upset, but Joe needs to see your mom. Danni wants to see her too."

"Well, you all go have a good time with her, then."

"I thought maybe we could all go to dinner together."

Sarah got up from the table. "I'm going to bed."

Matt grabbed her wrist. "Sarah."

She tried to pull away, but he pulled her down on his lap, squeezing her, caressing her with those big hands. "Sarah," he whispered, "don't be angry."

"Let me go, Matt. I'm disappointed with you. I'm disappointed with everyone. This family almost fell apart four years ago because of her, and now we're all supposed to pretend it never happened."

"No. You're wrong. No one is pretending it never happened. But you need to meet with your mom, Sarah. You need to let her see the girls. She needs to understand what she lost by walking out."

Tears rolled down Sarah's face. She was angry with herself for crying. Matt wiped them away.

"Don't you see, Sarah? It's a chance to lay everything out on the table. She's going to see a family that didn't fall apart. Because of you, Sarah. You kept the family together. You kept Danni from losing it. You kept Joe in school, and because of you he has a future. You got Abbie and Aimee through the bad times."

Sarah buried her face in Matt's shoulder. "You stepped up to the plate and accepted the responsibility. You kept the family whole, Sarah."

Matt took her by the shoulders and turned her to face him. "Oh, Sarah, don't you get it? The family didn't fall apart. Everybody made it through. Because of you."

"Oh, Matt. How could she do that to us? How could she just turn her back on her family?"

Sarah wept and curled up against Matt and thought, *What would I do without him?*

They sat like that for some time; then Sarah got up and blew her nose.

"You're wrong, you know. It's thanks to you she has a house to go home to," Sarah said. "And you were the one who insisted that Joe stay in school. You were the one who paid for everything. She should thank God that she has you for a son-in-law."

They put the lights out and made their way upstairs.

"I'll check the rugrats," Matt whispered.

Later, Sarah lay curled against Matt, who snored softly. *How can he be asleep as soon as his head hits the pillow?* she wondered. Her own thoughts were all over the map. *I'll never sleep*, she thought. Matt's words were laying heavy on her mind, as were Abbie's. But reliving the anguish of those first few months made her heart ache. Sarah not only had the girls to worry about but Danni and Joe as well. Danni was due in a few weeks and falling apart, and poor Joe was in his second year of college and wondering where the money was going to come from. Losing Dad was hard enough on him, but having Mom run out on them was devastating. He'd shown up on their doorstep one night.

"I'll just drop out of school and get a job. I don't know what else to do." He looked forlorn, thin, and worried. He hadn't slept for days. His college payment plan had left for Europe without a word.

Matt took Sarah aside. "He needs to stay in school, Sarah. The worst thing that could happen to that kid would be to drop out of school. He needs... normalcy."

"What am I supposed to do, Matt? We don't even know when or if Mom is coming back, but her accounts are closed to us. If she wouldn't come home for the birth of her granddaughter, she obviously doesn't care if Joe finishes school or not."

"Then we have to pay, Sarah."

He was insistent.

"We can call it a loan. The girls have college funds. We need to keep him in school, to complete this term. Then we can help him get loans to go on. He can live in your mom's house this summer and work at the dental office, but we need to keep him in school."

Sarah couldn't believe that her mother had missed Joe's graduation. As months and years passed, marked by life events, Sarah would think, *I can't believe she would miss Lucie's birth; I can't believe she would miss Abbie's first communion; I can't believe she would miss Aimee's first day of school; I can't believe she would miss the birth of Jack; I can't believe, I can't believe.*

Finally, she just stopped pondering. And stopped jumping every time the phone rang.

The family stopped asking one another, "Have you heard anything?" Mom was gone.

Abbie finally stopped crying herself to sleep. Now it was going to start all over again.

Sarah finally drifted off for a fitful sleep. The alarm went off at seven a.m. She felt for Matt, but he was already out of bed and in the shower. She went down the hall to wake the girls.

The morning was uneventful. No fights about Grandma or outfits. Abbie was subdued. Sarah packed lunches and put cereal and juice on the table.

Matt came downstairs and spread kisses all around. Sarah curled her hands around a cup of coffee. Looking down into her coffee cup, she said, "Maybe we'll have Grandma over here for dinner Saturday with Aunt Danni and Uncle Rob and Uncle Joe and Christine."

Sarah heard only silence. She looked up to find Abbie smiling at her. "Thanks, Mom," she said.

"I don't remember Grandma too much," said Aimee.

"That's okay." Matt reassured her. "You'll get to know her again."

It was Sarah's turn to walk Matt to his car. "You're a gem, Sarah girl." He touched her face.

"I'm going to have lunch with Danni. We'll make some plans. Call me later. We'll meet up at Abbie's game."

The girls were more animated when Sarah walked back inside, and she hustled them around in time to catch the school bus. Then she climbed the stairs to shower for the day. Sarah hoped she was doing the right thing.

DANNI 2005

SECRETS AND REVELATIONS

The alarm at the Morales household went off at five thirty. Roberto Morales had to leave at six fifteen in order to make it to work by seven a.m. He took his job very seriously. They were barely keeping their heads above water, and having a solid income and benefits meant they would stay afloat. Rob was rewarded last year with a promotion to assistant manager of the new-car service department at the dealership.

Danni stretched and rolled on her side, taking time to get out of bed to try to thwart the nausea she would feel as soon as she was upright.

Rob walked into the bedroom from his shower and gave her a morning kiss. The sight of him still made her weak in the knees, even after all these years.

"Still tired, babe?" He stroked her hair. She smiled up at him and stretched. "Why don't you stay in bed until the kids wake up?"

"No. I'm coming. I want to make you breakfast."

"No, no. I'll just make some toast and coffee."

Danni got up anyway, put on her robe and slippers, and wandered down the hall, pausing for a peek at the kids on the way.

Rob was making coffee, and the smell made Danni want to wretch. She pulled some saltines out of the cupboard and nibbled one.

"Coffee?" Rob asked her.

"No, not this morning. I'm meeting Sarah for lunch to figure out this 'Mom' thing after Jack's appointment."

"Hey, if you want to see your mom, you see her. You do what you want to do. Okay?"

Danni shrugged. "You know we owe Sarah a lot, Rob. It's just hard to know what to do. I have to take Sarah's feelings into account. I just have to."

Rob paused, sat down in a chair, and took her hand. "I'm serious, Danni. No one knows more about what we all owe Sarah and Matt, but if you want to see your mom, you need to see her. I mean it. I know how you always let Sarah boss you around."

"You don't understand." Danni shook her head. "Growing up, it's just…I don't know how to explain it."

"This might be your only chance to see your mom, Danni. This might be the only time she'll ever see her grandkids. Do you want to risk that?"

"No. I will see her. I just hope that Sarah feels the same way."

"You worry too much. Are Mom and Pop gonna keep the kids?"

"Yes. Why don't you let me fry up some eggs for you?" she asked.

"No. You sit down. I'm going to leave a little early; you know, we were swamped yesterday, and we didn't get everything out on time. You kiss the kids for me and tell them I'll see them later. And call me after Jack's appointment. Let me know how it went."

Danni walked him to the door after filling his thermos with coffee. "Will you be home early?"

"I'm gonna try. Try and keep the kids up for me, huh?"

"Sure."

Rob enfolded Danni in his arms. He kissed her head and whispered against her ear, "I love you."

Danni heard the kids stirring around when the door shut. She started taking oatmeal and brown sugar out of the cupboard. She would have to get them going soon.

Jack had a doctor's appointment at nine. Then she planned to take them both to Grandma and Grandpa Morales' before her lunch date with Sarah.

Both kids were fussy when she got them dressed and at the table for breakfast. Jack was whining about the doctor, crying, "No doctor! No doctor!"

Lucie was complaining and whining about having to go to Jack's appointment. "Why can't you take me to Grandma and Grandpa's house first?"

"No, Lucie. I'm not driving you to Grandma's then driving back after Jack's appointment. You're just going to have to go with me!"

Next year, Lucie would be starting kindergarten, and Danni would be starting all over again. The thought of

more doctor bills, diapers, and baby things made Danni worry. She was not in the mood to be a patient mom today.

This whole pregnancy thing was heavy on her heart and mind. They were quickly outgrowing the small ranch they lived in, but there was no money for a larger home. Jack was doing much better now, and this was the year Danni was going to look for work to keep food on the table, but now she was pregnant.

There was nowhere for the kids to play inside or out, and Jack was a busy toddler. She had hoped that by working they might save a little each month and could look for a bigger place.

So much for dreams. She should be used to having her hopes dashed. Danni hustled the kids around and headed for the doctor's.

The office was crowded, and they didn't get called back until nine thirty. Then they spent another fifteen minutes waiting in the small cubicle. Danni had a difficult time keeping the restless toddlers in check.

Dr. Webber felt that Jack was doing very well and could start regular yearly visits. He was almost in the normal percentile for height and weight. His vocabulary was normal for a two-and-a-half-year-old.

Danni thanked him, paid another office call co-pay, and piled the kids back into their car seats.

She got to the Morales home at ten thirty. Elena and Pedro Morales lived in a small gingerbread-style house on a large lot in the run-down neighborhood where Rob had grown up. He was the youngest of six children, a change of life baby who was a surprise to Elena.

Pedro was a gardener by trade, long retired, and their backyard was an oasis in a dingy neighborhood. He often walked the children through the grape arbor in the cold, crisp fall and would hoist them on his strong shoulders so they could pull off the sweet purple grapes. Apple, cherry, and peach trees lined the back fence. Raspberries, strawberries, and vegetables were cultivated and enjoyed year round from the freezer. The only patch of ground not covered by beautiful flowers or edible food was home to a sturdy old swing set, an old-fashioned jungle gym, and a sandbox.

They lived simply off a modest social security income, and Elena did sewing and alterations to supplement their income. They ate whatever they grew and helped out their neighbors and their church.

Elena canned corn, beans, beets, peppers, potatoes, tomatoes, and carrots. She made wonderful homemade Mexican dishes as well as jams, jellies, sauces, and salsa. The small home was always filled with the aroma of good cooking. Baked goods always lined the kitchen counters because Elena always expected someone to drop by.

And no one ever left hungry. How Rob grew up in such a home without being overweight was beyond her. Elena was truly the quintessential grandmother, and Danni always felt good about leaving the children, as she knew they would be loved and safe.

"Grandma! Grandma!" The kids ran toward the front door, where Elena stood, arms outstretched. They were smothered with kisses and hugs. Pedro swept Jack up in his arms.

Elena wiped her hands on her apron and proceeded to smother Danni with hugs and kisses. "Daniella, come. I have coffee on."

"No, Mama, no." Danni placed a hand protectively over her abdomen. "No coffee. Hi, Papa." Danni kissed Pedro on the cheek. "Thank you for taking the kids. Sarah and I need to talk about our mother."

Elena stared at Danni's abdomen with a knowing look. Not taking her eyes from Danni's midsection, she pointed to the kitchen. "Pedro, take the children to the kitchen; there's cookies."

Now she looked up at Danni's face. "You go, sweetheart." She walked with her to the door. "Remember to keep forgiveness in your heart, Daniella."

"Thank you, Mama." Danni kissed her good-bye. "I won't be late. Rob's going to try to be home early."

"I'll have dinner packed up for you when you get back."

Danni smiled. As she drove to the restaurant, she thought how lucky she was to have such great in-laws. No wonder the kids loved to visit them. The Morales home was a haven of love and comfort.

When Jack had to have his heart surgery, Elena and Pedro not only took Lucie, but also took care of Abbie and Aimee so that Sarah could stay with her at the hospital. They were wonderful people.

Danni touched base with Rob on her cell as she headed for the interstate. He was pleased and relieved that Jack had a clean bill of health.

"Now you can enjoy your lunch with Sarah. Give her a kiss from me, but don't let her boss you around, okay?"

Danni smiled. "Okay."

Sarah's favorite restaurant was a long way from the neighborhood where Danni and Rob lived. She was already there when Danni arrived, waving from a secluded back booth.

The girls embraced. "I've missed you," Danni said.

Sarah squeezed her hands on the table. "You look tired."

"Well, so do you," Danni retorted.

Sarah shrugged. "It's the graveyard shift. Five nights a week I'm up all night; then the others I try to live and sleep like a normal person. But it's great for the girls and home life. I'm home in the morning before school and home most nights to tuck them in."

"How are my girls?"

"Oh, Abbie is driving me crazy. And Aimee is taking lessons."

Danni laughed.

"I swear, Danni, she's like a devil child some days. But the two of them together, well..." Sarah shook her head. "So many times I look at them and think that's you and me all over again."

"They do remind me a lot of us."

"How about Lucie and Jack? You said he had an appointment today?"

"It went well. He's in the percentile parameters they want him at. He only needs to see the cardiologist every year now."

Sarah smiled. "Oh, Danni."

"I know. I'm so lucky. Lucie is fine. She's ready to start kindergarten."

"I ordered us a glass of wine."

Danni looked at her lap. "No wine for me. Water is fine."

"What do you mean? You don't want any wine, Danielle? How are we going to get through this lunch talking about mom without getting half-smashed?"

Suddenly, Sarah stopped and stared.

"Baby sister, you're pregnant!"

Tears welled up in Danni's eyes. The waiter was approaching their table, and Sarah waved him away.

"Danni." Sarah leaned in and spoke softly. "It's okay. Babies are a wonderful thing. Abigail's not really a devil child."

Danni chuckled through her tears. Sarah took her napkin and wiped her sister's face.

"It's not a good thing. Not now. We can't afford this baby, Sarah."

"Oh, Danni. Is that what Rob thinks? I don't think so."

Danni sat quiet, twisting her napkin.

"You haven't told him, have you?"

"No. I don't know how. This was the year that I was going to get a job to actually use this fancy education to help us out. Now I'm going to be starting all over with diapers and midnight feedings. It's just not a good time."

"Is Rob's job okay?"

"Yes, he's really doing well. But we're still catching up from Jack. Our health benefits just aren't the best. I mean, that almost wiped us out. We're outgrowing the house, and without me working, there's no hope of getting a bigger one."

"Danni, why don't you let Matt and me help out?"

"No." Danni smacked her palm on the table. "No! You've helped us all out way too much. No. No. No. We'll be okay. I just hate to let Rob down."

"Rob is crazy about you, Danni. I've never seen anyone so crazy about someone. He'll be ecstatic. Trust me. Things happen for a reason. It will work out."

Danni sniffed. "I really wanted to start working this year."

Sarah waved the waiter over. The girls ordered salads and a breadbasket. Sarah told him to leave both glasses of wine. "I'm sure I'll need them if we're discussing mom."

The breads arrived warm and crusty with small pots of butter.

"Comfort food." Sarah smiled, buttering her bread. "Elena will be thrilled to have another grandbaby to spoil."

"She didn't seem thrilled. She seemed concerned."

"You told your mother-in-law before you told Rob?"

"No. She just took one look at me this morning and she knew. She's a Mexican witch with intuition like you!"

The girls laughed. Danni felt so much better sitting there with Sarah, her secret out. They enjoyed their salads, and each sat quiet with her own thoughts for a time.

"Danni, why don't you give Joe a call?"

Danni looked confused.

"I mean, both of you were always the math whizzes in the family. There may be something, some kind of accounting or auditing work you could do from your home. Like contract work. You have a decent computer. You might have to invest in a fax, but it's worth a try."

Danni's face brightened. "I will."

"Joe knows a lot of people. And Christine is an attorney. Who knows? It's worth a try. I'll ask Matt too. You know how Joe did the accounting for the dental office when he was in school."

"Sarah, you're a genius." Danni felt better than she had in weeks. "But we still need to talk about Mom."

Sarah groaned. "Oh, do we have to? I was really enjoying myself."

"Yes. We have to."

Sarah sighed. "I'm going to have a dinner Saturday night. I'd have it Friday, but she doesn't get in until seven something. By the time they get through baggage and home from O'Hare, it will be late for the kids."

Danni smiled. She sighed with relief. "Oh, Sarah. Thank you. I was worried you'd be angry with me for wanting to see her. I couldn't bear having you angry at me right now."

"Oh, I'm not happy about it, Danni. Matt browbeat me into it. But the way I see it, Mom owes us a lot. She owes Matt a lot and she owes Rob a lot. Thanks to them, she has a home to come to."

Danni stared out a far window. "I do want her to see my kids. It's important to me that she meets the grandchildren she walked out on. I don't know that I'll even want her to stay around, but I want some kind of explanation. Maybe I'll never understand why, but I feel that I deserve it. We all do."

"I don't really know how I'll react when I see her. I don't know if she'll be changed. I know I am. But I really worry about Abbie and Aimee. She hurt them bad once, and I don't want her to hurt them again."

The sisters sat silent for a time, each reflecting on old memories, old hurts. Sarah took a couple of sips from the second glass of wine then pushed it away and shrugged. "Better not. I'm driving."

They discussed small details, like the menu, what Danni could bring, what time they should arrive. Sarah looked at her watch. "I'm going to call Joe when he gets off work. I'm sure he and Christine will be there."

The girls finished their lunch and chatted about the kids. Danni could tell that Sarah wanted to say something but was hesitant. "Why the quiet? Talk to me."

"Danni. I have some other things to tell you. But now I'm worried about upsetting you. Especially now." She stared out the window.

Danni looked concerned. "What?"

"I went to the house the other day. I found out some other things about our parents that we didn't know."

"Like what?"

Sarah cast her eyes down and shook her head. "Maybe this just isn't the right time. I just wanted to discuss it with you before anyone else."

"Don't do this to me." Danni reached across the table and took her hand. "You have to tell me now."

"Mom and Dad didn't graduate from Northwestern. Their degrees are phonies."

Danni looked shocked. "No."

"And there's more. Mom was only sixteen when they got married, and she was pregnant with me."

Now Danni looked pale. "I don't believe it. She and Dad were so pushy about our education. Look how Dad acted when I wanted to get married."

"Have you told this to Matt or Joe yet?"

"No. Only you. But I talked with Mrs. Bloom for almost two hours. I was late getting home for Aimee, and it caused a huge fight with Matt. Mrs. Bloom confirmed everything. Mom was sixteen when she got married."

"That means she's only ... fifty-two." Danni paused. "Wow."

"Well, Dad was twenty-four when they got married. Talk about robbing the cradle. Mrs. Bloom described it as date rape. She also said that our grandparents probably were a murder-suicide because our grandfather didn't want to acknowledge me."

Danni leaned back in the booth, incredulous. She didn't know what to say. Her entire life had changed in a moment's time. Like Sarah, Danni felt her whole life had been a lie. "My God. No wonder Mom was so messed up," she whispered.

"Don't make excuses for her, Danni," Sarah chided. "She had everything. Dad gave her everything, and when he died, we would have all been there for her. You know that."

"Oh, Sarah. Mom was never the strong one emotionally. Dad was. You feel that way because you're much like dad. Everything was always easy for you. I think this explains a lot of mom's behavior."

"Oh, rubbish, Danni. She abandoned all of us because it was easier, that's all. She took the easy way out."

"I don't agree. If Mom was really just sixteen when she married Dad, he was probably pretty controlling. You know how he could be. I don't think Mom would have been complicit with the deceit."

"Mrs. Bloom felt the same way, but I disagree." Sarah shrugged.

Danni was full of questions and curiosity, much as Sarah herself had been. So she fielded her questions as honestly as she could. Then she glanced at her watch.

"Well, baby sister, I have to run. We don't have any groceries in the house, and Abbie has a four o'clock game."

Danni reached for the check, but Sarah shooed her away. "No way." She shook her head firmly.

"At least let me leave the tip."

"No."

Danni kissed Sarah on the cheek. "That's from Rob."

"That's what I needed. A kiss from a hot Latino." They embraced, Sarah holding Danni tight for a moment, feeling protective of her little sister. "I am looking forward to having my family over for dinner. And congratulations about the baby. When are you going to break the news?"

"Probably at dinner, when everyone is there."

The sisters went their separate ways, promising one another not to let so many weeks go by without having lunch together.

"Don't forget to call Joe about work," Sarah reminded her.

"I won't. It's a good suggestion. It can't hurt."

Danni drove in silence, so she could think. Wasn't it just like Sarah to offer help? Danni wondered what would have happened to her when Mom left if Sarah hadn't been there for her.

The shock of her mother disappearing without even a good-bye had been tempered by faith. Danni assumed her mother was grief stricken and was certain to return home before the baby came. She kept watching the road and waiting by the phone, reassuring everyone and herself that Mom had only gone on a sabbatical. She'd never miss Lucie's birth. But Mom didn't show up. And Danni's faith was shattered over and over.

Danni's faith was restored briefly when she made plans for Lucie's baptism. Surely, Mom would never miss the baptism. And once again, Danni's faith was shattered when yet another milestone in Danni's life passed without her mother.

Sarah and Matt were godparents to Lucie. And also to Jack. And Jack was another story altogether. Danni shook her head.

DANNI 2005

MEMORIES

Danni's memories were often associated with scents. Her mother wore Tabu cologne. Daddy would take them shopping for it when they were little on Mother's Day, her birthday, or holidays. She and Sarah often made fun of it when they grew up.

"Mom! You can afford good perfume now. Why do you wear that cheap stuff?" they would ask.

"Why, you girls bought me that set when you were little," she would say. Or "Joseph got that perfume for me. I love it because it came from you."

Sarah and Danni would fall out laughing.

Her mother was an early riser, and Danni would recall awakening and finding her mom sitting at the picnic table outside, with the newspaper and her coffee. Her kisses

always smelled of coffee and Juicy Fruit gum and her hugs the familiar scent of Tabu.

Mom always used Tide laundry detergent, and Danni couldn't use any other brand now. And when Sarah got old enough to go on sleepovers with her friends, Danni would lay in the dark, terrified, clutching Sarah's pillow so she could smell it.

She remembered her childhood as happy and her parents as loving, her father stern yet tender with her. She recalled times when he would often scold Sarah, who would stand boldly in front of him, hands on hips, while Danni cowered and cried because Sarah was "in trouble."

She recalled little of any kind of conflict; being a pacifist at heart, she subconsciously chose only peaceful memories to retain.

But there was one stain on her memory whenever she thought of her father. Sarah was thirteen and in eighth grade. She had lied to their mother about going to Kristen's house after school to work on a science project.

"Don't tell." She shushed Danni. "I'm going to the mall theatre with Jeremy Stacy."

Her mom started getting concerned when she hadn't heard from Sarah by dinnertime and called Kristen's mother. Then it was one frantic call to her dad.

He had not been happy to hear from her mom.

Danni, frightened beyond words, hid in her room and lay on her bed.

The door had slammed open, and Danni trembled when she saw the look of smoldering rage on her father's face.

"Where is she, Danielle!" he shouted, grabbing her roughly by the arm. "I'll give you one chance to tell. Do not lie to me!"

"She's at the mall theatre with Jeremy Stacy." Danni sobbed.

Her father threw her back on the bed and stormed out of the house, while her mother screamed after him, "Jack! Jack!"

Danni cried into her pillow.

It was less than an hour later when they pulled in the drive. Later, Sarah would tell her that Dad had found them holding hands coming out of the theatre and physically dragged her to the car.

Danni could see the rage in her father when he brought Sarah into the house. The girls didn't know he had been drinking but knew they'd never seen him in this state.

He took off his belt and began hitting Sarah. Sarah fell to the floor and covered her head from the blows raining down on her. Danni and little Joseph screamed and sobbed in terror. Their mother also screamed and pawed at their father.

"Stop, Jack!" she cried. "Stop! Enough! Please stop."

Danielle's father, who always seemed so in control, could not seem to get control. He would later cry to Claire that he was tormented by his own demons and he knew what could happen to young girls.

He finally stopped and stood over Sarah. "Don't you ever lie to us again" was all he said. Then he dropped the belt and walked outside.

Mom lifted Sarah up, both of them crying. She helped her upstairs and into her pajamas. Sarah was covered with red welts over her legs and backside.

Danni felt she had betrayed her sister. She crawled into bed with her. "I'm sorry, Sarah." She sobbed. "I didn't mean to tell."

"It's okay, Danni. It's okay." Sarah held her in her arms. Danni would never forget.

Later that night, Daddy came into the room. Danni wasn't sound asleep. He smoothed Sarah's hair back. "I'm sorry I hurt you, Sarah." His voice full of remorse and pain. "But you mustn't ever lie to us again. I just can't tolerate that."

"Okay," Sarah whispered.

"I love you, Sarah."

"I love you too, Daddy."

Sarah had taken a beating but won the battle.

Danni could see the change after that terrible night. Daddy was home at dinnertime every night and spent lots of time with them. He started giving Sarah more freedom to do things with friends, and as Danni reflected on her childhood, she realized he was allowing his oldest to grow up.

CLAIRE 2001

Claire gazed down at what was left of Jack. The only sound was the *whoosh*; then the *click* of the ventilator. Jack was barely recognizable. He was bloated, with tubes and wires going everywhere and tape across his face holding the endotracheal tube secure.

"Mrs. Bradley." The doctor put his hand on her shoulder. "Mrs. Bradley. I'd like to speak with you. Will you come?" He gestured toward the door, and Claire followed meekly down the hall to a conference room.

"Coffee?"

"No."

The neurologist settled into one of the hardback chairs. He seemed uncertain how to start.

"Mrs. Bradley, I know you're aware of the severity of your husband's condition. His CAT scan revealed massive bleeding within the brain." He looked at her closely to see if she was following. Then he continued. "I believe recovery is not possible." The neurologist sighed and

leaned toward Claire. "The brain loss has been significant. His kidneys have lost function; you can see he is not making urine."

Claire looked up at his face.

"Mrs. Bradley, we would like to do an EEG, and if there is no brain activity, as we suspect, we would advise you to consider taking your husband off life support."

Claire blinked and grimaced. The doctor continued.

"I realize how difficult this is for you. But you must consider your husband's quality of life." The doctor paused and sighed heavily. "I also would have you consider donating your husband's viable organs."

Claire made eye contact with the doctor. She could see the anguish this conversation was causing him. She held up a hand to stop him.

"I'll agree to the EEG and let him go if you recommend it. I'll talk with my children about the organ donation."

The doctor looked surprised and relieved. Most spouses were ruled by their emotions and unable to make an informed decision upon the initial conference. This woman seemed so in control and unemotional.

Claire stood up. "If that's all, I'm going back to my husband."

"Of course." The doctor rose. "I'll order the EEG for tomorrow morning."

"Oh," Claire added, "our children will be here soon. If you could speak with them as well. Our oldest daughter is an RN and knowledgeable."

The doctor nodded.

Claire walked back into the ICU. The nurses looked at her sympathetically or simply averted their eyes. She

could see Matt, Sarah, and Danni at the bedside. The "only two people at the bedside" rule was ignored by the staff and Jack's family.

Danni was holding Jack's hand. "Daddy, we'll get you home soon. You hold on."

Matt put his arm around Claire, who stood stiffly. "Rob is picking Joe up at school," he explained.

"They said you were meeting with the neuro doc. What's the latest, Mom?" Sarah asked.

Claire took a deep breath. "He suggested that I take your father off of life support. There has been a lot of damage."

Danni burst into tears. Sarah's jaw was clenched. She stared at her mother with smoldering eyes, Jack's eyes.

"That's absurd," she whispered. "Many people survive strokes each year. He can't be serious, Mom."

"They're going to do an EEG first."

Sarah literally leapt at Claire. "What are you saying? Are you saying that you gave him permission to kill my father?"

"Sarah!" Matt grabbed her arm. "Calm down."

"Calm down!" Sarah whirled at Matt. "I'm fighting for my father's life here, and you tell me to calm down?"

Sarah was trembling with anger. "I'm too young to lose my dad! Danni and Joe are too young!"

Claire continued. "He said the brain damage was significant. He asked us to consider organ donation."

Sarah knelt down in front of her mother. "Mom, I'm a nurse. I know about these things. Dad can survive this. He might have a rough couple years, but we can all help. We can't just let him go. You can't just let him go."

Claire laid a palm on Sarah's cheek. "Your father would not want to live this way."

The doctor entered the room. Sarah stood and glared at him as if she wanted to scratch his eyes out.

"Which one of you is the RN?" he asked.

"I am," Sarah replied.

"I would like to show you your father's CAT scan."

Sarah, Matt, and Danni followed the doctor out, making introductions as they walked.

As the children left for the viewing room with the doctor, Claire spotted the young blonde pacing back and forth outside the unit. Claire had noticed her there last night as well. She looked grief stricken and lost, staring into Jack's room, trying to catch a glimpse.

Claire approached the young woman, who panicked when she made eye contact with Claire and bolted down the hall. Claire pursued, calling after her, "Please stop. Don't run away. I know who you are, Gayle."

The stunned woman stopped in her tracks at the sound of her name. She turned to face Claire. "How do you know my name?" she whispered.

Claire stopped. A sad smile touched the corners of her mouth. "He often speaks your name in his sleep."

"I love Jack," Gayle spoke, squaring her shoulders. "I believe he loves me."

Claire reached out her hand. "I'm his wife, Claire. Can we go for coffee or tea?"

As Claire and Gayle settled down for a cup of coffee, Gayle spoke first.

"I know who you are too. There are lots of pictures; family pictures in his office. I don't mean to hurt you,"—

Gayle bit her bottom lip—"but Jack and I plan to start a life together. He loves me."

Claire slowly stirred cream into her coffee.

"Jack is dying."

The shock and fear etched on the young woman's face made Claire reach out to place an arm around her shoulders. She felt like a small girl. She couldn't be much older than Sarah or Danni. While Claire gave the young woman time to digest her words, she wondered at the irony of her own actions. *I sit here and give comfort to my husband's mistress, and I am bereft of emotion. I have no faith in myself as a wife and mother. Oh God, please restore my faith.*

Gayle's voice broke her reverie.

"No." She shuddered. "He can't be dying."

"Gayle," Claire spoke softly, "Jack has suffered brain damage, and the doctors have advised us to remove him from life support."

Liquid blue eyes welled with tears that spilled over her cheeks. "You can't do that. He promised. This year we were going to start our life together."

This year? How long had the two of them been together? Claire was filled with anger at the empty promises Jack had made to this young girl. She knew he had no intention of ever leaving her. This poor girl was no different from the dozens of other young, mostly blonde girls Jack had had affairs with during their marriage.

"Gayle." Claire spoke softly, but with authority. "I recognized you because you fit Jack's M.O. He has had many affairs during our marriage. He makes the same promises to all of them. Jack would never leave his family."

Now it was Gayle who became angry and defensively pushed Claire away. "I don't believe you! Jack loves

me. He said you would try to stop him. He hates you!" she cried.

Claire took a sharp intake of breath. The girl was probably telling the truth. Jack probably did say such vile things. Did he hate her?

Now Gayle could see the pain etched on Claire's face.

"I'm sorry." She sobbed. "I never wanted to hurt you. This is so hard. I'm just so frustrated that I can't sit by his bed and hold his hand. It's not fair."

"I know that." Claire sighed. "Gayle, I don't mean to hurt you either. But I want you to understand that you are not the first and probably would not have been the last. I thought that when Jack reached his forties his wandering eyes would focus on us, but when he continued to have liaisons outside of our marriage into his fifties, I realized that Jack would never change. You are a lovely young woman. You can't be older than our daughters."

"I'm thirty-four."

"Our oldest daughter is thirty-two. Jack is fifty-six."

"Jack always says age isn't relevant. It's attitude."

"How flippant of him."

Gayle sniffed. "I don't know what I'll do without him."

"Gayle, you have a whole life to live. You need to find someone closer to your age and single."

Claire thought that Gayle needed to see Jack. If she could see him, she might realize that Jack was dying.

"If you come back after eight, I'll let you have some time with him. But you must wait until my children are gone. They must not know. They'll head home to care for our grandchildren by eight."

Claire emphasized the word *grandchildren*. Gayle's eyes lit up for a moment.

"You'll really let me sit with him?"

"Yes. I think you need to see him. Jack would want you to be there."

Gayle reached out and hugged Claire. "Thank you. I'm sorry for the things I said. Jack never said he hated you. It wasn't nice. I'm so sorry."

Claire patted her. "It's okay. Come back after eight p.m., and the nurses will let you in."

Claire continued to sit and stare at her coffee after the girl left. "So much damage control, Jack," she whispered. "So much damage control."

SARAH 2001

THE AFTERMATH

Sarah's anger was almost as palpable as a black cloud. The doctor used a pointer to highlight areas of her father's brain as he droned on with his explanations and reasonings.

Sarah made the physician nervous. Her stance—arms folded across her chest—broadcast angry denial. She refused to look at the films up on the view box. He continued to focus on the main theme: "There is no hope of recovery."

"I see neonates recover from severe brain bleeds all the time," she interrupted.

"Is that your area of expertise?" the physician inquired of Sarah, who didn't respond. "Your scope of practice is neonatology?"

"Yes. And I've seen miracles."

101

"Ms. Law. Neonates' brains and your father's brain are not the same." The doctor laid his pointer down. "Neonatal hemorrhages can sometimes resolve, I agree, depending on the severity. This is not the same."

"I don't believe you. I don't believe this whole thing! You're giving up on my father, who is just about the strongest man I've ever known! Well, I'm not!" Sarah's voice was becoming shrill.

"Sarah." Matt put his arm around her, which she shrugged off.

The physician was puzzled. This was the reaction he had expected from the wife—denial, anger, clinging to false hope—but not from the daughter. Not from a medical person. The daughter was out of control, irrational.

"The EEG will tell us more."

"I think we should wait on the EEG," Sarah interrupted.

"Ms. Law, even with the vasopressors at the maximum dose, your father's renal perfusion is very poor. His kidneys are failing. You can see by his lack of urine output and his generalized edema."

Sarah shook her head no, tears welling up in her eyes.

"Your mother is in agreement that this is best for your father."

"I don't believe my mother is capable of making a rational decision at this point," Sarah spat at the physician, who appeared stymied at her behavior.

"Your mother seems quite rational to me," he responded softly. "You are the one who seems quite irrational."

Sarah looked to Matt, who stared at the floor tiles. No one spoke up for her. She ran from the room.

Matt found her in the waiting room, crumpled on a ratty sofa. He sat down beside her and wrapped his arms

around her. She made a halfhearted attempt of pushing him away. He didn't allow it.

They sat that way, silent, Sarah cradled in his arms like a child, large tears rolling from her face, for a few minutes. Matt reached over to a chrome end table where a box of tissues lay and pulled several loose for her. She wiped her eyes and blew her nose.

"You didn't say a word," she chided him.

"You said it all I think." He patted her arm. "I'm sorry, baby. I'm sorry about your dad."

Sarah sighed. "There's nothing else to do, I guess." She shrugged and squirmed loose from Matt's comforting arms. "But I won't be part of it; I won't. I won't go back in there and just stand by while they kill my dad."

"Sarah."

"No. I can't, Matt. I can't just watch it happen. He's my father."

"You need to say good-bye."

Sarah's eyes were resolute, but her posture was beaten. "My dad knows how much I love him. I don't need to go in there and hold his hand and tell him things he already knows."

"That doctor said the EEG is scheduled for the morning; then they'll take him off if it confirms what he says."

"I'll go back in tonight. I want to see Joe. He's going to be devastated. He's too young to lose his dad. I'm too young. And poor Danni. She's ready to deliver, and Dad will never see this baby." Sarah shook her head. "I'll go back in tonight, but I won't come tomorrow."

"Your mom will need you, Sarah," Matt reasoned. "The girls need to say good-bye to their grandpa. Danni and Joe are going to need you."

"Mom will be there. This is what she wants. Let her handle it."

"You don't mean that. Your family doesn't operate like that. And I've never known anyone more devoted to someone than your mom is to your dad."

"Go and get the girls. I'll let them see Dad tonight."

Matt hesitated.

"It's okay. I'm okay. Go get the girls." Sarah stood up, and Matt wrapped his arms around her.

"Cut your mom some slack, Sarah. This is just as hard on her."

Sarah glared at him but said nothing. She watched him go. She walked back to her dad's room. Claire and Danni sat on either side of his bed, holding his hands. Danni's face was swollen with tears. Sarah went to Danni's side and wrapped her arms protectively around her shoulders.

She made eye contact with her mom and saw the pain and grief etched there but said nothing. The three sat in silence for a time.

A few minutes after six, Rob walked in with Joe who, immediately dropped his backpack and gathered Claire in his arms. She stifled a sob against his shoulder. Then he hugged Sarah and Danni. Joe was pale and shaky. Sarah held his hand as he stared down at their dad.

"Rob said it was a stroke."

Claire put a hand on his shoulder. "He's not going to be okay, Joseph."

Sarah turned away and stared out the window. Rob stood behind Danni, hands on her shoulders.

Claire did her best to explain what the physician had said. Joe had a lump in his throat and found he could barely speak.

He looked toward Sarah. "Sarah, you're a nurse. What do you think?"

Sarah leaned her forehead against the windowpane and closed her eyes. "I want him to live, Joe. I want him to be okay. But he's not. And what I think doesn't really matter."

"It matters to me."

Sarah smiled. That was Joe, her baby brother, just twenty-one. "I think," Sarah whispered slowly, "that we need to see what the EEG shows, like mom said. And I think we all need to help each other get through this."

Claire was able to breathe. That was her Sarah. Always the leader. So much like Jack.

Claire started making little suggestions that the family should head home at about seven. Matt had arrived with the little ones, who had little understanding of what was going on, only that grandpa was "sick."

In their innocence, they giggled and roughhoused with Uncle Joe, whom they'd been more thrilled to see than Grandpa. Sarah had been scolding them to settle down, but they were antsy with boredom.

Joe was adamant that he would stay with Mom and ride home with her. In a panic because Gayle was coming, Claire took Joe aside and explained that she wished to have some alone time with Jack before tomorrow. He finally reluctantly agreed to go on ahead with Danni and Rob.

Everyone said their tearful good-byes and left around seven-thirty. Gayle arrived promptly at eight. Claire had been watching for her and went out to greet her. She took Gayle by the hand to the nurses' station.

"This is one of my husband's dearest friends, and I'm going to let her have some time alone with him."

The RN looked bewildered but said nothing.

Claire pointed her toward the door. "I'm going downstairs for a cup of tea. I'll give you about an hour, okay?"

A tearful Gayle nodded and went into Jack's room. Claire sighed and went to the cafeteria in search of herbal tea. She sat alone at a table, with only her thoughts for company.

She wondered what she would do without Jack. How could she possibly make a decision on her own? Claire leaned her head against the wall. She was guarding herself from the creeping fear of being alone with only memories of her failures.

CLAIRE 1974

DASHED HOPE

Claire's sense of anticipation was high. She alternately paced between the kitchen and the front window, cooking and watching for Jack. She had taken care to wear his favorite dress and dabbed cologne behind her ears and on her wrists. A pork loin she'd been saving for a special occasion now filled the house with a wonderful aroma.

Mrs. Bloom had kindly agreed to keep Sarah and Danielle for a few hours. Claire had bathed them early, dressed them in their pajamas, and bundled them next door.

Claire stared at the clock. Jack was late. The pork loin was ready, potatoes mashed, candles lit. The meat would soon dry out.

Claire nervously chewed her thumbnail. He had promised. After the last one, Jack swore there would never be another indiscretion.

Thirty minutes passed before she heard his car in the drive. Claire greeted him at the door. He had been drinking. Claire's anxiety rose. Jack wasn't usually a happy drinker. She could see from his face that the night probably wouldn't go as planned.

"Hey, baby." His words were slurred as he nuzzled her neck. "What are you dressed up for? We don't have to go anywhere, do we?"

Claire shook her head. "I just wanted us to have a nice, romantic supper."

"Where are my girls?"

"They're at Mrs. Bloom's, Jack."

Jack's face clouded over. "I like to see my girls when I get home. A man works all day; he likes to see his girls at the end of the day."

"Well, they'll be home soon," Claire chirped. "I wanted us to have some time."

Claire hustled around to get the food on the table. When she had everything ready, she looked around. Jack was gone.

Claire found him upstairs, taking off his suit. She wiped her hands on her apron. "Dinner's all ready, Jack."

"Hey, come here, beautiful." He gestured with his finger. Claire gingerly stepped over toward the closet. Jack grabbed her tightly and started walking her backward to the bed. "If the girls aren't here, we may as well take advantage."

Claire tried to push him away. "Dinner's ready, Jack. The roast won't keep. Let's wait, honey."

"I don't care about the roast." Jack was already pushing her toward the bed.

"God, you're beautiful." Jack was lifting her dress and pulling down her panties and nylons. Just as when she was sixteen, Jack's hands could be everywhere at once.

Claire protested and squirmed to no avail.

"What the hell's the matter with you? Are you frigid or what? You know, you get pissed off if I have sex with other women, but you aren't very willing when it's you I want."

Claire pulled him down on top of her. "I want you too, Jack. But I just cooked this special roast for you—"

Claire was unable to finish her sentence. Jack smothered her with kisses. "God, I need you, Claire. Forget the roast."

They sat down to dinner after everything was cold and ruined. Claire's pretty dress was a rumpled mess. Now Jack was tired.

"I'll make sandwiches with it tomorrow." He shrugged, pushing his chair away from the table. "I'm gonna lay down on the sofa while you clean up. Then I want you to go get the girls before it gets too late. They should be in bed."

Claire panicked. The evening was almost ruined. "Jack, I wanted to talk to you about something. It's important." She followed him into the living room.

Jack turned on the television. Without turning to look at her, he said, "So talk."

"Please, Jack," Claire pleaded. "I've been waiting all day to talk to you about this."

Jack looked at her face and sighed. "Okay, baby. What's wrong?"

Claire ran to the hall tree and picked up the folder she'd brought home from the school. With bright eyes and pounding heart, she handed it to Jack.

"It's for community college. The lady said I can take a test called a GED, and if I pass, it's like a way to get into college. Jack, I could take classes!" Claire was breathless.

Jack's expression wasn't good. His face was clouding over with anger. "Where the hell did you get this?" he asked her slowly.

"I was talking to Mrs. Bloom about being home all day, and she told me about this community college that accepts the GED test. I went and talked to a lady in admissions today and picked up some information."

"Just how many other people have you told that you don't have a high school diploma in this town?" Jack seethed at her.

Claire stepped back. His anger was like a black cloud. She hesitated.

"Just Mrs. Bloom and the lady at the college," she whispered.

"And just what do you think you'd do with the girls all day while you're chasing around at a college?"

"Mrs. Bloom said she'd help." Claire backed against the wall. Jack towered over her, and Claire was reminded of her father on their wedding day. She saw Jack's fist clenching, and her heart pounded in her chest at the anticipation, the expectation that he intended to slap her just as her father had.

"I could get a job to help us out." She breathed in and out, voice shaking.

Jack's rage exploded. "Oh, you want a freaking job!" he screamed. "Well, let me tell you what your job is. Your *job* is to take care of my children and my house! That's what your job is Claire. And you can't even do that right!"

Tears streamed down Claire's face, and she kept her eyes closed tight. She shrunk against the wall and cowered at the blows of his words.

"Do you think that'll help me at work, Claire? Huh? Do you? Do you think I'll be up for promotion when they find out my wife didn't even graduate from high school?"

As he leaned over her in his rage, Claire shrunk down against the wall. He reached out and roughly stood her up to him, shaking her until she opened her eyes. "Well, tell me, Claire. Do you enjoy humiliating me? Do you sit around thinking of ways to embarrass me?"

"No." Claire sobbed. "I love you, Jack. I just wanted to do something for me."

"Well, I'd like to do something for me too, Claire. But I can't because I have to make money to pay for the roof over your head and clothes for you and the girls. That's what responsible people do, Claire. Is that why I bought you that car to drive? So you could run around town telling people you're a dropout?"

Claire clung to Jack. "Jack, please." She sobbed. "I just wanted to make you proud of me."

"Do your job then, Claire. Go get my girls. That's what I want, Claire. I want you to be *here* when I get home, taking care of my children."

He gestured around the house. "This is your job." Jack crumpled the paper in his fist. "I don't ever want you to bring this up to anyone. I tell everyone that we met at Northwestern. I don't tell them you're uneducated. Do you understand?"

Claire was wracked with sobs. When she tried to slink down, Jack stood her up again. "Do you understand me, Claire?"

Claire nodded.

Jack shook his head. "I've never raised my hand to you, Claire. I'm not that kind of guy. But you almost make me lose control sometimes."

Claire's sobs were subsiding. She felt as though she were floating away. Her eyes looked blank.

"Claire," Jack went on, "from the first night we went out, I promised you I'd take care of you, and I have. Now, I know I've made a few mistakes, but I've kept my word. We took vows, Claire. All I want is for you to keep a good home and be a good mother. That's all I want, understand?" He lifted her chin.

Claire nodded.

Jack shook his head. "I think you need more to do around here. Maybe it's time for another baby." He hugged her tightly. He turned her around like a petulant child and patted her bottom. "Go get the girls now; it's about time for their bed."

Claire left the congealed roast and potatoes on the table, the candles burned down to nubs. She walked next door to get the girls. Mrs. Bloom took one look at Claire's swollen, tear-stained face and knew that things had not gone well. She said nothing, just gave the girls a hug and patted Claire's arm.

Claire immediately stiffened. "Thank you," she said quietly.

The girls were ecstatic to see their father, who roughhoused with them for almost an hour while Claire cleared away the dinner. When she called to them to say good night to their father, Sarah stamped her foot.

"We want to stay with Daddy!"

Jack wrapped his arms around her waist. "Home and family, Claire. This is what it's all about."

Claire put the girls to bed and stood in a steaming shower. She wished she could just melt away. Once again, she had made the wrong decision and disappointed the one she loved the most. Claire felt a failure. She couldn't make her husband proud of her or happy enough to come home each night.

Jack was in bed, turned away from her snoring. Claire curled up against his frame, vowing to be a better wife and mother. She had never felt so all alone.

Jack applied heavy pressure during the weeks following the argument to increase their family size. Claire resisted. Danni was just two. And Claire's body didn't tolerate pregnancy well. She was sick most of the nine months, lost weight drastically, and suffered from post-partum depression. Unable to deal with her bouts of morning sickness and melancholy, Jack's first affair came about when they were newly married. Claire, just sixteen, missed her mother and her home terribly. Jack had moved them far away, and he worked long hours in sales, leaving Claire alone for long hours of the day. He often came home to find her in bed crying, and Jack didn't handle her moods well.

"What do you want from me?" he would ask. "I have to work hard; I told you that. I come home, my dinner's cold, and you're in bed all the time."

"I'm sorry, Jack." Claire sobbed. "I'm just so lonely. I miss my mom."

Jack stared at her small frame curled up in the bed. She was such a child.

"Why don't you get up and fix yourself up a little, and we'll go out. We'll go down to the Embers, have a drink."

"Jack, I'm not supposed to drink. And it's so smoky in there I don't like it. Can't we just stay here?"

Jack was busy pulling out a dress from the closet. He ignored her and picked out heels, walked over to the bed, and sat her up and pulled her shirt over her head. The sight of her swollen breasts caused him to pause. "Claire, you are so beautiful."

Suddenly his train of thought changed. Jack was unbuttoning his trousers.

"No, Jack. Please. I don't feel good."

"Shh." Jack pushed her down on the pillow. He took off his shirt and pants and pulled her panties down. "Let me look at you," he whispered.

Jack's breath smelled of alcohol, and when he lay on top of her, she caught the scent of a woman's perfume, which made her nauseous.

When they finished, Claire got up and began to hang things up as Jack snored softly in the bed.

She wondered who he'd been with as she pulled her nightclothes back on and went downstairs. Jack seemed to have an insatiable appetite.

Claire, who had never cooked before, was trying to learn. Her kitchen was not stocked well, as Claire was never sure what she should buy. Jack had taken her to the store several times, and they had thrown a lot of things in the cart, along with a cookbook. Claire enjoyed trying new recipes but frequently lacked essential ingredients and would add them to the ever-growing list.

She pulled cold chicken and potatoes from the fridge and started warming a plate. Jack probably wouldn't sleep through the night and would awaken ravenous.

Meeting her neighbor Mrs. Bloom had been a God-send for Claire. She was about the same age as her mother and had a son away at college. They met outside one day, and friendly Mrs. Bloom took Claire under her wing.

"Goodness. You're just a child and left here all alone all the time!"

Claire opened up to Mrs. Bloom, and for the first time since her marriage, started getting dressed and looking forward to the day ahead. Mrs. Bloom took her shopping, gave her cooking lessons, and kept her company.

"For heaven's sake, why don't you go and visit your mother? She's probably as heartbroken as you are!"

"Oh, Jack would never take me. And I'm not sure if my father would want to see me."

"We should call her."

Claire stared. "What?"

"I said we should call her, Claire."

"Call my mom?"

"Haven't you even talked with your mom since you've been married?"

"No."

Mrs. Bloom took her in hand and walked straight to her phone.

"Call your mother."

Claire stared at the phone, remembering her father's words. Mrs. Bloom laid a reassuring hand on her shoulder. "Go ahead, dear. Dial."

Claire's heart pounded while the phone rang.

"Hello?"

"Mom."

Claire heard a muffled sob. "Mom, I miss you." A tear slipped down Claire's cheek. "You should see my belly. It's getting huge."

"Claire, your father's in the yard. He hasn't been working much; his health is bad. He can't find me talking to you," she whispered.

"Mom, I want to see you. I want you to see the baby."

"Give me your number, Claire. I'll call you when I go to the store."

Claire recited her phone number. "Will Papa let me visit?"

"I don't think so. I will try to talk with him. Are you happy? Good. I love you, Sarah."

"I love you too, Mom."

Claire replaced the phone on the cradle and nestled into Mrs. Bloom's comforting arms.

"Now we need to teach you how to drive!"

Claire looked up bright eyed. "Drive?"

"Yes. I'm going to have Mr. Bloom give you driving lessons. He worked at the school when our Samuel was there."

That night, Claire was behind the wheel, with Mr. Bloom in the passenger seat, driving up and down through her subdivision.

Mrs. Bloom was standing in the door waiting for Jack when he arrived home.

"Hello!" He waved.

"Jack," she called to him. "Can you come here for a few minutes?"

Jack strode across the yard.

"Come in." Mrs. Bloom smiled and settled Jack at the kitchen table. She noticed his eyes were glassy and he'd been drinking. At twenty-four, Jack was already gaining around the middle.

"Some coffee?"

"No thanks. I stopped off for a few beers on the way home." He shrugged. "Helps me unwind."

"Yes." Mrs. Bloom's intense stare made Jack uncomfortable.

"If Claire's been bothering you too much, I'll talk to her," he said.

Mrs. Bloom looked incredulous. "Why, that child couldn't bother anyone if she tried! She's the dearest creature on God's earth."

Jack smiled. "What can I do for you then?"

"Claire needs more money for the household budget."

Jack's face clouded over. It was obvious to Mrs. Bloom what a volatile young man he could be. She worried about Claire.

"Has she been discussing our finances with you?"

"Don't be ridiculous. I'm the one who takes her to the store and appointments, Jack. No one could run a household on what you give her."

Mrs. Bloom leaned forward and placed her hand over his. "Jack, you want Claire to be a good wife. Then you need to be a proper husband. What preparations have you made for the baby?"

Jack blinked.

"Babies require a lot of care. And they require all the things necessary to provide that care. You need a bed, layette, bottles, formula, clothing."

"I never thought about it."

"Jack, I realize that you're a young man. And I understand that you grew up without a mother to teach you these things. But Claire has needs too. To start with, you need to start coming home at a decent hour. Think about the amount of time she's left alone. And she needs to learn to drive, and she should have a car."

"A car!"

"Jack, babies go to the doctor a lot. Your life would be easier if Claire had a car and could drive herself around. It would give her a sense of freedom."

Jack appeared to be thinking. "Can I have a cup of that coffee?"

Mrs. Bloom patted his hand, stood up, and poured a hot cup for Jack. "Mr. Bloom gave Claire her first driving lesson tonight. He used to teach driving at our Samuel's school."

Jack quietly sipped at his coffee.

"Claire is becoming a decent cook. She'd love to entertain, make friends, invite your coworkers over; but she has to borrow a lot from me because her kitchen is not properly stocked. And she needs the proper cooking utensils, pots, and pans. She needs dishes to entertain with. She could make a proper home for you and this baby. She just needs help."

Jack looked down at the table. "I appreciate everything you've done for her."

"She idolizes you, Jack. She wants to make a good home for you."

He nodded. "I'll start giving her more money. She should have told me."

"She doesn't find it easy to talk with you."

"There's been a lot going on at work." He sipped at his coffee. "It just seems she's never happy."

"Claire needs to see her mother. She's trying to go it alone, and she's scared. If Claire can work things out with her parents, you've got to take her to see her mom, Jack."

"That bastard of a father hit her the day of our wedding. I'd like to kill the S.O.B.—sorry for my language."

"It's time to put that behind you now. For Claire's sake."

"I'll try."

Mr. Bloom came into the kitchen. He was a strapping man in his early forties. "Any of that pie left?"

Jack stood up. They shook hands. "Jack."

"You gave Claire a driving lesson. How'd she do?"

"Pretty good. For a woman driver that is." He winked at Jack. Mrs. Bloom swatted him with the dishtowel. She set a huge piece of pie down in front of him. Jack found his mouth watering.

"I've wrapped up a couple pieces for you and Claire, Jack. But I know she's been working on supper for you, so I want you to take them home for dessert."

Jack thanked them both and walked home with the pie thinking of all Mrs. Bloom had said. He did want all of those things she'd talked about. If a little extra money would make Claire happier, he could handle that. The house did smell good. Claire was in the kitchen and had spaghetti ready for him.

He wrapped Claire in his arms. "So, my girl's gonna be driving."

Claire smiled, delighted.

"I'm sorry I haven't been a better husband, Claire. I'm just as new at this as you are."

Claire's face beamed with joy. She smothered him with kisses. Jack raved about her spaghetti, and together they curled up on the sofa with Mrs. Bloom's blueberry pie.

JACK 1969

LESSONS TO LEARN

For the first time, Jack started making plans for the baby. He set Saturday aside for nursery shopping.

After Claire made them breakfast, she left the dishes on the table and left for a day of shopping.

When they came home loaded with bundles and layette items, Jack dumped everything off in the living room and pulled Claire toward the stairs.

"No, Jack. I have to clean up. The dishes need washed."

"They'll be there tomorrow," he said as he pulled her up the steps.

"Jack, the doctor says I shouldn't have sex after the seventh month."

Oblivious to her protestations, Jack pulled her into the bedroom and lifted her dress over her head.

Later, they lay side by side. With Claire's increasing size, she was having difficulty finding a comfortable position.

"If you can work things out with your parents, we'll take the baby for a visit."

Tears rolled freely down Claire's face. "Thank you, Jack."

The weeks ahead were filled with happiness for Claire. She threw herself into her driving lessons and cleaned and organized like a madwoman at home.

Jack kept his word about being a better husband and came home on time most nights. He painted the nursery yellow, put together the baby bed, and with the help of Mr. Bloom, carried the dresser upstairs.

With the aid of a friendly clerk, Claire had picked out bottles, diapers, formula, and clothing necessities. Jack surprised her and brought home a beautiful quilt set from his coworkers. The nursery was ready, and Claire was pleased.

After five weeks of driving, Mr. Bloom took Claire down for her official driving test, which she passed with ease. Smiling, Claire held her new driver's license in her hand. "I did it!"

"Well, I guess it's official. I put another woman driver on the road!"

He let her drive them home. "Do you kids want to come to supper?" asked Mrs. Bloom.

"No, thank you. I really want to surprise Jack. I'm going to cook a special supper for him to celebrate."

Jack phoned as Claire was preparing dinner.

"I can't make it home, babe. I'm really sorry. I'm up to my neck in paperwork, and if I don't get it done, I'm gonna have to work late all next week."

"Oh, Jack. I was making a special dinner."

"Claire, you know we talked about this. There's nothing I can do. I'll be home late, so don't wait up."

"I love you, Jack."

"Yeah, me too."

Claire stared at the phone as it clicked off. Just then Mrs. Bloom tapped at the door. "I brought you kids a couple pieces of cake for dessert," she said when Claire opened the door.

She saw the disappointment on Claire's face. "What's wrong, dear?"

"He has to work late at the office. He's loaded down with paperwork."

"I'm sorry, dear." Mrs. Bloom patted her hand. "I know he's been trying really hard." She stepped to the door then turned, a smile on her face.

"Why don't you take my car, Claire? I mean, if he can't come home, surprise him with a romantic picnic at the office!"

"Oh, do you think I could?"

"Of course. Why don't you get ready and pack up a nice supper, and I'll bring the car over."

Claire was excited and felt like she was going on a date. She ran as fast as her pregnant body would allow up the stairs and picked out her prettiest shift. She touched up her makeup and hair and put some perfume behind her ears. Mrs. Bloom helped her pack a small basket full of essentials and dinner for two.

Claire had only been to the office building once but remembered where it was. It was on the main drag downtown. She parked in the ramp and took the walkway into the lobby.

"Can I help you?" asked the security guard at the desk. "The offices are closed, miss."

Claire held her basket out. "I'm bringing my husband dinner. He's working late."

The security guard smiled. "Do you want me to ring him up—let him know you're on your way?"

"No." Claire waved. "I'd like to surprise him."

Claire's heart fluttered as she rode up to the twenty-sixth floor. The offices of Halderman & Wells were dark and deserted.

There was no receptionist to greet her. Claire made her way to Jack's office. The anteroom was dark, his secretary's desk empty. But lights were on behind the frosted glass door. Claire heard moaning...and other sounds. Sounds she recognized.

Horrified, she stood frozen. Slowly, she reached out and turned the knob. The sight that greeted her was so shocking Claire could only stare.

A half-empty bottle of liquor sat between two glasses and an array of takeout containers on the coffee table. The sofa was strewn with Jack's shirt and sport coat and a woman's shirt, bra, and panties.

Jack's secretary, Wendy, was bent at the hips over Jack's desk, which had been cleared off. Her skirt was bunched up around her waist. Jack stood over her, his hands on her hips.

She lifted her head up with a shocked expression as the door swung open. With the flat of his palm, Jack pressed her head back down on the desk. Claire saw her lick her lips and smile. Jack never broke the rhythm of his thrusts.

"Go home, Claire," he said breathlessly, eyes glassy. "You shouldn't have come. Go home."

Claire ran from the office dropping the basket from her grasp. At the elevators, she fell to her knees and wretched with dry heaves.

She crawled into the elevator and pushed the button for the lobby. Claire couldn't get the picture from her mind. It was as if a photograph had been imprinted there.

The security guard watched the ghostly pale, pregnant girl walk toward the ramp annex. "Everything all right, miss?" he called after her.

Claire made it to the car, fumbled with the keys, and fell into the seat, where she was wracked with sobs. Wendy was almost old enough to be her mother.

Claire didn't remember driving home or dropping the car off at the Blooms'. Pale and shaking, she sat on the sofa and waited.

CLAIRE 1969

BROKEN SPIRIT

It was 1:00 a.m. when Jack came home, smelling of booze and sex.

He pointed his finger at Claire. "Don't look at me like that. You shouldn't have come down there unannounced. I told you not to wait up." He dropped the picnic basket on the table.

"I want a divorce," Claire announced calmly.

"Don't be ridiculous. I'm going to bed. Clean up that mess." He pointed to the picnic basket.

Claire ran to the table and picked up his car keys. She was almost to the door when he roughly grabbed her. She kicked and punched at him, and when he wrapped his arms around her and dragged her up the stairs, she tried to scratch his eyes.

Sobbing and crying, Claire seethed. "I hate you!" she hissed.

Jack threw her down on the bed, slammed the door, and shoved his car keys in his pants pocket.

"Stay in that bed, Claire. I swear if you get up..." His voice trailed off. "I'm gonna sleep on the sofa. We'll talk tomorrow when you're calmed down."

Claire cried into her pillow until sleep overcame her. She awakened to the sounds of Jack in the shower. She felt for his keys in his pants pocket, but they were gone.

Jack walked out of the bathroom, towel drying himself. He stared at his disheveled wife, her face tear streaked and swollen.

"I'm sorry, Claire."

She noticed he was covered with scratches and bruises. She wondered how many were from her. "How could you do such a thing, Jack?"

He sighed. "She doesn't mean anything. It was just sex. You know I love you. I would never leave you, Claire. No one compares to you."

Claire stared at him.

"Look. We were working and took a break to order some food and had a drink, and it just happened."

"How many times?"

"What?"

"How many times did it happen? I mean, did you start out on the couch and move to the desk? I just know that once is rarely enough for you, Jack. And you were there very late."

"Look. I'm sorry. It'll never happen again. I promise."

"I want her gone."

Now Jack looked alarmed. "Wendy?"

"Yes. Wendy. I want you to fire her."

"Claire, I can't fire her for that. She's a good secretary. I'll never touch her again."

"I swear, Jack. You can't keep an eye on me twenty-four hours. I swear you'll come home one day and I'll just be gone. I want her out of our lives."

"Okay. You win. She's gone. Monday morning. Claire, I can't lose you."

Claire continued to punish Jack with scathing looks all weekend while he continued touching, petting, and atoning for his actions.

Claire called the office Monday afternoon, heart pounding. Wendy was gone. The phone was answered by a Mrs. Downing.

That day something was delivered to Claire, along with a large bouquet of flowers. It was a beat-up turquoise 1965 Chevrolet Bel Air sedan. It was the most beautiful car Claire had ever seen. Along with the flowers there was a note from Jack: "From this day forward, your freedom. Love, Jack."

THE FIRE 1969

Claire felt a sense of power she'd never felt before after the Wendy debacle. But it was short lived. After a long and difficult labor, Sarah was born a week later. She came screaming into the world on a crisp December day, announcing to everyone that she had arrived.

Claire's seventeenth birthday came several weeks later. Jack was delighted with his daughter. He doted on her, talked to her, walked the floors with her.

Sarah was almost a month old when Claire heard from her mother. "You can come. He's not happy, but I told him I might as well be dead if I couldn't see my daughter and granddaughter. I'm knitting her something special for Christmas."

Claire was so excited she called Jack at work. "We'll talk about it when I get home."

They made plans to go home to Montpelier the following weekend. Claire confirmed things with her mother then spent the week getting ready.

Jack just couldn't drive fast enough Saturday morning to suit Claire. She was so excited to see her mom and to show off Sarah.

The street was cordoned off when they arrived. It was crowded with fire trucks, police cars, ambulances, and onlookers. Thick black smoke made it difficult to see. A policeman was waving them off.

Jack started to turn around.

"No, Jack!" Claire frantically rolled down her window to yell at the policeman. "My house is down there!" She pointed. "My parents are expecting me."

"What is your address, miss?" The policeman looked in the car and saw Claire holding the small baby.

"Twenty-one fifty-six Primrose," Claire responded.

The policeman's face looked stricken. "Please, sir," he spoke to Jack, "just park right there. I'll be right back."

Jack felt dread. He looked at the anxiety etched on his young wife's face. The policeman returned with an officer in a suit. He leaned in.

"Hello, folks. I'm Detective Cole. There really isn't a good place to talk around here." He looked around.

"Are my parents okay?" Claire asked woodenly.

"I'm sorry, missus. There's been a fire. A bad one. Several firemen were injured trying to save them. I'm so sorry."

Claire fell forward in a faint. Jack grabbed the baby as the detective ran around to the passenger side and gently leaned Claire back against the seat.

"There's a motel up on Route Nine." The detective told him. "Your wife needs to rest, and I'm going to need to talk to you both later."

The next few months went by with Claire in a fog.

She had little memory of her parents' funeral mass. The horror of hearing the policeman tell them they suspected murder-suicide and that the fire had been deliberately set caused Claire to withdraw into a shell.

What have I done? she wondered. *I've killed my mother. If I'd left her alone, she'd still be alive.* Claire barely spoke or paid any attention to Sarah.

Jack took care of everything—the funeral mass, the church dinner. The fire marshal was a close friend of Claire's father and a member of their parish and ruled the fire as accidental for the sake of the church and insurance.

Jack did what needed to be done for the burial—obtained death certificates; found insurance policies, cash, and other valuables in a safety-deposit box; and hired an attorney since Claire was only seventeen.

They learned that Claire was considered an emancipated minor because of her marital status. She and Jack were entitled to everything. The house was a total loss, but insurance covered rebuilding on the property, and they made a tidy profit on the sale a year later.

Claire remained unresponsive and mute most of the time. She would feed Sarah if Jack prepared the milk and placed the baby in her arms, but when Sarah cried in that tiny motel room, she didn't seem to notice.

They'd been gone two and a half weeks when they returned home. Jack was desperate to get back to work. He worried about leaving Claire alone. And he worried about Sarah being cared for.

He went to Mrs. Bloom. She was shocked at the tale he told.

"That poor child. She never got to see her mother. He made sure of that."

Mrs. Bloom stayed with Claire for two weeks. The second Friday evening, she made Jack sit down. "Jack, Claire needs help. She's in a terrible depression."

"I don't know what to do." He placed his head in his hands.

"Claire needs a doctor. This has hit her hard. She needs more than I can give her."

"You mean a head doctor?" Jack looked up. "No. We don't want to do that." He shook his head. "No way. I can't have people I work with finding out. She'll get over it."

Jack would not be swayed. Mrs. Bloom came back the third week. She talked softly to Claire, who seemed to walk around functioning at a limited level in a daze.

"Claire, you must snap out of this. Sarah needs you. You've suffered a terrible loss. Do you want to lose Jack and Sarah too?"

Claire's muddy eyes cleared for a moment. "No."

"Jack is trying to hold things together, but he can't do it alone. Claire, you need to try. You need to come back to us."

Little by little, Claire did. She quietly watched Jack interact with their daughter. She'd never seen two people so connected. Claire came out of her shell slowly, started taking the initiative to answer Sarah's cries and offer warmth and comfort.

But the bond between mother and daughter would never be the same. Sarah would never respond to her mother in the same way again. She had become her father's child and would remain so for many years to come.

It had been more than ten months since the fire, and Claire seemed to be back to her old self. She was only seventeen, but Jack always told people she was twenty-three.

She was planning her first dinner party. It was to celebrate Jack's promotion at work to vice president of Midwest sales operations. Claire had been poring over menu ideas while Sarah happily crawled all over the floor. Claire was pregnant with number two.

Already four months along, her doctor had scolded her. "You body hasn't even had time to recover." He shook his head.

Jack was nervous about the party. He wanted everything to go smoothly. He suggested having a professional caterer.

"No, Jack!" Claire groused. "I want to do this."

Jack also worried about the house. They had a lot of money from her parents, and Jack had suggested moving to a larger home.

"No. I want to stay here. I like the neighborhood."

Jack knew that Claire didn't want to leave Mrs. Bloom.

"Then we'll add on and remodel."

The kitchen was filled with pamphlets, fabric and paint swatches, and blueprints. He wished it were already done.

Saturday night came, and even Jack was impressed with Claire's efforts. The decorations were elegant, and the food smelled wonderful.

She had baked six pies, all from scratch, with Mrs. Bloom's help. She also baked a torte, a cheesecake, and a sheet cake decorated with "Congratulations, Jack!"

Jack had set up a bar in the living room, and people started filtering in at about five thirty for drinks and hors d'oeuvres.

By six thirty, the house was filled with happy chatter and tinkling glasses. Sarah was bundled off to Mrs. Bloom's after meeting everyone.

"She's such a beautiful baby, Claire!" cried Mrs. Downing.

Claire smiled. "Thank you, Ruth."

Dinner was served buffet style, as their house was too small to seat everyone.

The party guests raved about the food and the desserts.

"Claire baked everything from scratch." Jack beamed with pride.

Jack's boss stood up to make a toast and to congratulate Jack and his wife on the promotion. "And for those who don't already know, Jack will be representing Halderman & Wells at the Las Vegas Expo on the eighteenth. Let's wish him every success!"

"Here! Here!" Everyone drank to Jack. Claire was pleased but wary about the Las Vegas trip. She wandered in the direction of Jack's boss, who kissed her cheek and congratulated her personally on the success of her party.

"When did you decide to send Jack to Las Vegas?" she queried. "He hasn't told me anything about it."

"Shame on him. Actually, I've had him in mind for some time. He's a shrewd negotiator, that husband of yours."

"How long will he be gone?" she asked.

"Four days. He asked about taking you along, and I said sure, but he was worried about you traveling with your condition."

Claire heaved a sigh of relief. "Well, you picked the right man for the job. He's very motivated and has strong convictions. I think that comes from his service in Vietnam."

"Where was he stationed, dear?"

Claire paused and thought about it. "I don't remember. I don't know if he even told me; we weren't married then."

"Who was in Vietnam, our Jack?"

"Yes," answered Jack's boss. "I just found out myself."

Tom Reynolds, one of Jack's coworkers, seemed animated. "I'll have to find him. Find out if we were on the same side and all that."

They laughed.

Later, as she was carrying an empty tray to the kitchen, Jack grabbed her by the arm and pulled her outside. "What in the hell's the matter with you, Claire!" he hissed so no one would hear. "Telling people I was in Vietnam. How am I gonna get this smoothed over? Now they all want to know about Vietnam."

"But you were in Vietnam," Claire whispered innocently. "You said you served fourteen months over there. You told me."

"I just told you that to get in your pants! I never left the States. Grow up, will you?"

Claire stared numbly.

"I wish you'd never open your mouth!" he hissed. "Just don't talk to anyone else." He threw her arm off him and walked back into the house, leaving Claire alone outside.

She hugged herself against the chill night air. Jack had lied about Vietnam to get in her pants, and it worked. He'd been in her pants ever since.

135

Claire stepped inside, head down, and walked into the kitchen. Mrs. Downing was scraping, rinsing, and stacking dishes.

"Oh, thank you, Ruth," she said. "You don't have to do this."

"Oh, Claire. I love to help out. Are you okay, dear?" She looked at Claire, concerned.

"I'm okay. I was just surprised by the Las Vegas announcement. I just can't travel right now, and I wish I could go."

"Oh, I do too. But traveling is hard on me at my age too. So when Mr. Bradley asked if I would mind working for Mr. Reynolds so he could take Wendy along, I felt the same way. Glad I didn't have to go, but wishing I could."

"Wendy?"

"Yes. Mr. Reynolds' secretary. You may have seen her before. Tall, blonde. The artificial blonde, you know what I mean?" she said, leaning in. "With a large bosom."

Claire felt an old, familiar nausea creeping up. Jack had never "disposed" of Wendy. He had just moved her out of sight.

Claire's heart thudded achingly in her chest. She felt as though her life was falling apart once again.

By the time the party guests said their good-byes and filed out, Claire had settled back into her shell somewhat.

The party had been a huge success, and Jack felt bad he had snarled at Claire.

"Hey, I smoothed over that whole Vietnam thing, so don't worry about it, hon."

She ignored him and carried dishes to the kitchen.

Jack followed her to the kitchen, leaned on the doorjamb. "Why don't you let that go? Let's go upstairs, have our own celebration."

"I'm going after Sarah," Claire said as she untied her apron.

Jack grabbed her by the wrist and pulled her close. "C'mon, baby. Sarah can wait a few minutes."

"Why don't you call Tom?"

Jack stared, confused.

"Maybe you can borrow Wendy."

Jack stepped back. "What are you talking about?" he whispered. His face looked stricken. "Claire, there's nothing between us. I swear."

"I'm leaving you, Jack."

"Claire." His face bespoke his shame. Even as she spoke the words, Claire realized they were empty threats.

There was nowhere for her to go. She was seventeen, uneducated, with no income, no family, or friends, and pregnant with a ten-month-old. What was she to do, move next door with the Blooms?

It suddenly all became too much. Claire collapsed on the kitchen floor.

"Claire!" Jack screamed, falling to his knees beside her. Claire felt she would drown in her tears. There was no lifeline for Claire, no way out. This was her life.

Jack held her and rocked her. "I'm sorry. I'm sorry." He kept repeating the words. "Please, Claire, forgive me."

THE LOSS

Claire lost the baby that week. The doctor, rather than scold Jack, scolded Claire once again.

"I warned you," he said, finger pointed threateningly at her face. "Your body needs time to recuperate. Either use some self-control or birth control!"

Jack left for Las Vegas the following week. Claire felt drained, empty, and alone and was left to wonder what Jack was doing in Vegas. He swore he wouldn't take Wendy, swore he was through with her.

Claire ignored him. She tried to turn to Sarah for comfort, but Sarah preferred her father and Mrs. Bloom.

When Jack returned home, he found his things in the spare room. The gifts he attempted to lavish on Claire were ignored. Only Sarah was filled with glee to see him.

Now toddling around the furniture and gnashing at her new teeth, Sarah was becoming the light of Jack's life.

Claire was back to walking woodenly about the house. "Alive but not living," Jack would tell Wendy.

Sarah was fourteen months old when Jack knocked at his wife's door. "How long are you going to shut me out of our marriage bed?" he asked.

Claire tried to run away, but Jack roughly grabbed her. "Claire, I'm going crazy here. I'm home with you, but you're not here! I can't take much more of this punishment!"

"Leave me alone, Jack."

"No. I won't leave you alone. I love you. Just you, Claire. It's always been you."

A tear ran down Claire's cheek.

"Oh, baby. I can't bear to be apart from you anymore."

Jack slept in the bed that night and every night after. He promised that he would never be unfaithful with Wendy again.

And Jack kept his word. Wendy had given him an ultimatum. She'd had enough of her role as the "other woman" and wanted more. Jack was unwilling to give her more. He made it clear to her that he would never, ever leave Claire.

Wendy left the company, and Jack made sure that Claire knew. He felt relieved to have it all over. Wendy had started to get too serious, nagging, and demanding, and he was a married man. Besides, there was someone new with the company—a young blonde, fresh out of high school. Her name was Amber.

And she had caught Jack's eye.

JACK 1972

DECEIT

Danielle was born in early 1972. Their lives had resumed a peaceful coexistence.

Jack's feelings for Danielle were different than for Sarah. As much as Jack shared a special connection with Sarah—her being Jack's girl, outgoing, independent, confident, and strong—Danni was more like Claire: petite, dark haired, clingy, and timid. Jack felt protective of Danni, who would always be his baby.

He handled her tenderly with care and fatherly love, always scolding Sarah if he thought she was too rough or loud around the baby.

Jack was careful in his relationship with Amber. He never wanted to hurt Claire again. Claire and the girls were his world. But Amber was like a rich dessert after a

sumptuous meal. He just couldn't resist the temptation. And there were so many temptations around.

Jack loved having a young girl again. His relationship with Wendy had become a drag. Amber was willing and easily manipulated. Her innocent naiveté made it easy for Jack to exploit her feelings.

He was careful to stagger his late nights at work and only took Amber out occasionally. He had sworn fidelity to Claire and really didn't consider what he was doing with Amber straying, as there was no emotional attachment on his part.

They stopped for a nightcap at a small out-of-the-way pub one Friday after a liaison in the office, when Jack laid eyes on Donna Frances. She was petite and brash. He couldn't stop staring at Donna's backside as she bent over the pool table, holding court with half the bar.

She had white, even teeth, long blond hair, and a tattoo high on her left breast, which she showed off by wearing a low-cut top.

She would throw her head back when she laughed, exposing her soft, white neck. Jack found himself lusting after her. He couldn't wait to dump Amber off out front with cab fare then rush back into the bar.

He didn't even know the girl's name, but Jack was mesmerized. He sent a drink over to her, waved, and smiled, but his was one of many and she merely nodded at him.

Jack asked the bartender her name.

"Oh, that's Donna Frances. She's a wild one, that one."

Donna hooked up with a large guy Jack wasn't about to mess with. He was angry that his drink and smile elicited so little response.

Donna left the bar with the big guy soon after, and Jack left for home. He couldn't chase the girl from his thoughts, and it made him morose and out of sorts when he arrived home complaining about his job, his cold supper, and the messy house. Even Sarah couldn't bring him out of his black mood.

"Claire, I never see you in anything but those old pants. Why don't you fix yourself up a little?"

Claire didn't answer. She rarely did anything right if Jack had been drinking, which was frequently. She prayed each night for God to make her a better wife so Jack would want to come home to her.

Jack went to bed lusting for the elusive girl at the bar. He went back each night hoping to see her, but she didn't return. He would drink in anger, as if the girl was betraying him.

Amber, confused at Jack's sudden disinterest, spent the week crying at work.

Claire knew something was up when Jack stayed out every night for a week, and she retreated into her shell.

Finally, Donna Frances showed up at the bar on Friday night, a black lace top seductively showing off her tattoo, tight pants hugging her curves.

"I understand you've been looking for me." She sidled up to Jack at the bar, showing off those white teeth.

He filled his senses with her scent. Jack was obsessed with the unknown of her. He felt himself falling into another abyss and was helpless to do anything about it.

If someone had just asked him, he would have, of course, told them that he loved Claire—no one else compared. But he couldn't help himself. Jack had to have this girl no matter what. And for the next four years, she

consumed his every thought and action, and she almost proved to be the undoing of his marriage to Claire.

They weathered the storm once again, this affair taking its toll on Claire and Jack as well. For years the name "Donna" would haunt Jack's dreams and Claire's sleep.

The marriage survived these rocky years, as it always did, Claire suffering through two more miscarriages before she became pregnant with Joseph.

Jack and Donna eventually came to an end. It was Donna more than Jack who wanted to move on. Jack vowed he was through with other women, he would never stray again, that Claire would be the only one forevermore.

CLAIRE 1973

THE GUILT OF FAILURE

Claire listened and knew she was hearing just another empty promise that Jack was incapable of keeping. And she resigned herself to this life she had accepted.

She blamed her own inadequacies for Jack's infidelities and felt helpless to overcome her imperfections. She turned to the church for guidance, and she was counseled to pray, to keep her marriage vows sacred, and to forgive her husband.

Their home grew, along with Jack's success, and Claire and the children wanted for nothing. Jack had truly listened to Mrs. Bloom and made sure Claire had plenty of money for the household. He lavished gifts upon her, encouraged her to use interior decorators, to buy whatever she needed to make their home a showplace.

Jack joined the country club, and golf became a new obsession. Claire felt that a dark period in their life was ending.

She was still bothered by the community college nightmare that had hit hard. Every time she thought things were better, there would be something else. Claire was unable to find the key to a happy marriage.

Jack was coming home early every night. He had slowed way down on his drinking. He surprised Claire with a large package one night.

"Open it up!" He beamed.

Claire tore it open and stared. It was a diploma from Northwestern. With her name on it.

"What is this?" she asked.

"Well, you wanted a college education. Now you have one." He shrugged, smiling. "I told you, I'll always take care of your needs."

Claire was horrified. "I don't want it!"

Jack was visibly upset. "Well, I don't want people at the country club finding out my wife's a high school drop-out!" he bellowed.

Danni started to cry. Jack lowered his voice. "It's okay, Claire. People do this all the time. It matches mine."

"It's dishonest."

"Grow up, Claire. You're almost twenty-one years old."

Jack hung the diploma up in the den next to his own. Claire refused to look at it.

She continued to protect Jack throughout their marriage and went to great lengths to hide his affairs from their children.

Sarah, most of all, had a hero worship of her father and always questioned Claire as to his whereabouts.

When she was only seven, independent and strong willed, Claire remembered her standing at the window watching for Jack.

"Sarah, it's eight o'clock. You have school tomorrow. Dad must be working late again. You need to go to bed."

Sarah had turned toward her mother, hands on hips. "Why are you mean to Daddy?"

"Sarah, I am not mean to your dad. I told you. He's working late."

"Daddy never comes home on time anymore. Because of you." Angry tears sprang from her eyes.

"Sarah." Claire shook her head. She went to Sarah and wrapped her arms around the defiant little girl. "Baby, Daddy loves you. He loves me and Danni too. That's why he works so hard."

"You make Daddy sleep downstairs. Sometimes he's sad. I heard him on the phone. He was telling someone you don't make him happy." Sarah sobbed in Claire's arms.

"Listen, baby." Claire held her daughter close. "Coming home to all of us is the most important thing in the world to your daddy. I don't know what you heard, but Daddy and I love each other, and we are happy." Claire wiped Sarah's eyes. "And most importantly, Daddy loves his girls."

"Why does he sleep downstairs sometimes?"

"Because he worries a lot about work, and he doesn't like to keep me awake."

Sarah stopped crying.

"Now you need to go up to bed, and I'll send Daddy up as soon as he gets home."

Later, Claire met Jack at the door. She could smell cologne on his jacket. "Jack, you need to spend more time at home."

"Claire, I'm really not in the mood."

"Jack," Claire interrupted. "It's Sarah. She heard you on the phone talking with someone. Talking about us."

Jack looked stricken.

"She cried herself to sleep."

"We have to at least make a show of things. She's getting older and starting to question why her father doesn't come home many nights."

"Claire." Jack's eyes were red and full of regret. "What should I do?"

"End it, Jack." Claire turned toward the stairs. "Whoever it is this time, end it."

Sarah would always be full of questions, and years later she pressed her mother with questions about their college years and how they met.

Claire was always vague and distant, full of excuses about not having time to discuss it.

CLAIRE 2005

THE HOMECOMING

The long overseas flight had come to an end, and the tired passengers anxiously fidgeted in their seats as the plane taxied to its docking space.

The senior flight attendant gave a stern warning on the overhead to "stay in your seats with your seatbelt securely buckled until the plane comes to a complete stop," which was ignored by some passengers who were already in the aisle reaching into the overhead bins.

"Apparently, rules don't apply to them." Jim Connell leaned toward Claire and extended his hand. "It's been a pleasure flying with you."

Claire smiled and took his hand. "Thank you, and likewise." Claire's heart was thudding, and her stomach fluttered as she exited the plane at O'Hare. She got in line at customs and went through the security process. It had

taken her a long time to get a new passport. Iris and Dr. Diebel had been invaluable in helping her re-establish her identity.

Her eyes kept scanning the crowd, even though she knew now that people weren't allowed down to the gates. If anyone had planned to meet her, they would be beyond the security screeners.

Claire sighed. "I'm really here," she whispered to herself.

She wondered if anyone would show up. With trepidation, she started walking with the other passengers like lemmings toward baggage.

She spotted Joe first. How like his father in his stance. He looked so much like a man. At the realization of it, Claire stopped in her tracks. *My*, she thought. *Joe has changed into a man.*

She watched him as she started walking again, running his fingers through his sandy blond hair, one hand in his pocket jingling his keys or pocket change, just like Jack always did.

Matt stood next to him. Her sweet Matthew. Of course he would be here. Claire couldn't have wished for a better son-in-law. Matt caught her eye from far away and pointed for Joe toward where she walked.

They both approached, Joe unsure of himself. Claire dropped her carry-on, started to extend her arms, and then hesitated, extending instead her hand. "Joseph." Tears glistened at the corners of her eyes.

"Mom." Joe took her hand, pulled her timidly toward him, and hugged her stiffly. "You look good."

"Joseph, you're a handsome man now." She turned toward Matt.

"Thank you for coming, Matthew."

Matt smiled. He grabbed her in a big bear hug. "Claire, you're a sight for sore eyes. I'm glad you came home." Matt picked up her carry-on, and the threesome continued to the baggage carousel.

"Long flight?"

"Yes. Desperately."

The three settled down on a metal bench and sat quietly while they waited for the luggage. So much to say, yet unable to say much.

"I'm gonna bring the car up; we're parked a ways away."

"I'll go." Joe practically jumped from his seat.

"No." Matt glared at Joe. "You stay with your mom. You two can talk."

Matt took off, and the two were left in silence.

Claire stared at the floor. "It's okay if you don't know what to say, Joe."

"I don't know what to say, Mom," Joe said as he stared at the floor. "It's been a long time; I know that."

"Are you all done with school?"

Joe stared at her. Claire was taken back by his look—part confusion, part anger.

"Yes, I finished school. Thanks to Matt and Sarah. They paid for the rest of the term the year you left, and then they helped me with loans, you know."

Now Claire looked shocked. "They paid for your school? But I don't understand, Joe. Your dad had set up a college fund; your schooling was completely funded."

Joe's face clouded over; the face of his father. "Mom, when you left you were just … gone. None of us had any access to any of your accounts. Don't you realize that?"

Now Claire stared at her son in disbelief. She blinked. "No. I didn't think. I just thought you'd be taken care of. I'm sorry, Joe."

"You don't need to be sorry to me. I got along fine. Matt and Sarah took care of everything. They took care of your house too. Matt's been paying the taxes and the upkeep for all these years."

It was a good thing that Claire was sitting down. Her head was reeling. All these years, and she'd never once thought about finances. Ever since her identity had been re-established, the sanitarium had been negotiating a fee with her insurance. She'd just assumed that the kids could get the money Jack had left and sell the house.

"Anyway," Joe continued, "I have a good job, and I plan to pay Matt back everything plus interest."

"And Danni?" Claire asked.

"She's fine. Danni has two kids now. Lucie's four and a half, and Jack is two."

"Jack?" Claire looked up.

"Jack Bradley Morales." Joe smiled. Claire looked wistful. A tear ran down her cheek.

"Jack would be so proud," she whispered.

Joe shook his head. "Dad would be yammering about his Mexican grandson having his name."

"He really did come around to Rob," Claire said.

"Yeah, he liked him. But he still liked to give him a hard time. Rob's a great guy, though. Danni's pretty lucky."

Claire's luggage appeared, and she and Joe pulled each piece off the carousel just as Matt pulled up outside. They loaded Claire's things and all piled in, Claire up front with Matt.

"I had the cleaning people come and take the covers off the furniture and put some sheets and linens out," Matt told her. "We stopped and picked up a couple things—bread, coffee filters, cream, butter, sugar, milk, eggs, and oatmeal for morning. Toiletries and things."

"Thank you, Matt. You remembered I like my morning oatmeal." Claire smiled. "It seems I am greatly indebted to you."

"Well, you know, Claire, families look out for one another. I never had that in mine, so I appreciate it in Sarah's."

"And you, Joseph? Is there anyone special in your life?"

"Yes, you'll meet her at dinner tomorrow night. Her name is Christine."

"She's a hottie, too," Matt added. "I don't know how this ugly mutt ever got a date."

Joe slapped the back of Matt's head. Everyone laughed and settled in with small talk.

An hour and twenty minutes later, they pulled up at the house. The night air was damp and cool, and the sky was lit with a million stars. Matt had lit the inside and outside lights. Mrs. Bloom stared from her front window.

"Do the Blooms still live next door?" she asked. "They have to be in their seventies."

"Yes," Matt answered. "They both help look after the house."

Claire stared hesitantly.

"It's okay, Mom. Everything's pretty much the way you left it." Joe took her arm.

Matt unlocked the front door and placed her luggage in the foyer. Claire glanced at the hall table and saw her dead cell phone still lying where she'd left it.

The house had a familiar heaviness, an oppressiveness that seemed to weigh her shoulders down. Matt busied himself in the kitchen, putting the milk away and setting out the coffeepot. "Claire, I know it's late and you're exhausted, but would you mind if I brewed a couple cups of coffee for the drive home?"

"Of course not. I'm going to go upstairs and change out of these clothes."

Claire stood at the top of the stairs. Looking down the hall, she hesitated then walked purposely to her bedroom. She felt Jack everywhere. He was everywhere yet nowhere. She placed her hand upon the mattress where they had lain together for so many years. The ache in her heart was so great! "Oh, Jack!" she cried out in her mind. "Why did you have to leave us? I just couldn't do it without you."

Claire undressed, unpacked her toiletries, and showered. The cleaning crew had placed freshly laundered towels on the racks and sheets on the bed. She let the hot water stream over her aches and pains and wash away her tears.

She put on some warm, comfy flannel pajamas, brushed her teeth, and made up the bed. She found blankets and the comforter packed in storage bags with scented sachets. Then she went downstairs to join Matt and Joe at the kitchen table.

"Feel better?" Matt asked her.

"Yes. I'm sorry I was so long." Claire poured a glass of milk and sat down. "Matt, I really am sorry for what I've done to you."

Matt shook his head. "I know you're full of regret, Claire. It's written all over your face."

She then turned to Joe and took his hand. "Joseph, no apology could suffice for what I did to my family. I'm not offering it up as an excuse, but rather an explanation of what happened. I wasn't myself when I left. I mean, I thought I was in control, but I wasn't."

Joe started to interrupt. Claire stopped him.

"Please, Joseph, let me finish." She hesitated, took a breath. "I had a mental breakdown. A collapse." Claire stared at the table and picked her nails. "I tried to kill myself. I have no memory of it, but I was told that they found me in the bath. I have the scars to prove it." She held out her wrists. "I was in a sanitarium in London for a long time. I had shock treatments and was on drugs. I had a lot of therapy to get me back to here."

Tears streamed freely down Claire's face. Joe felt his hardened heart melt a little. He squeezed her hand. "It's okay, Mom. It's okay."

"I came back to ask each of your forgiveness. And I will understand if you can't. It was a terrible thing I did. A terrible thing." Claire stifled a sob. "I had to leave. I had to."

Matt stood up and grabbed a box of tissues. Joe placed his arm around those small shoulders he was once so familiar with. "Mom," he said softly, "don't cry. It'll be okay."

Claire looked up into his face. "Can you ever forgive me, Joe? Can you?"

"Yes, Mom. I forgive you."

It came out so easy that Claire was at a loss what to do. Those three words lifted a heavy weight off her heart. She blew her nose and wiped her eyes. "I wanted a chance to talk with the girls too. I hoped they would come."

"Danni wanted to," Joe explained, "but it's hard for her with the two kids and Rob always working. She said to tell you she'll be at Matt and Sarah's tomorrow."

Claire looked to Matt, who shrugged. "Oh, c'mon, Claire; you know Sarah. It's like living with Jack most of the time. She's just so stubborn, strong willed, and difficult. I believe she'll come around; who knows."

Claire yawned and sniffed.

"Joe, we need to clear out. Your mom's tired."

Joe stood up. He hugged his mom. "We'll pick you up for dinner."

"No, no. I'll just drive over."

"There's no insurance on the vehicles," Matt explained. "Rob's been starting them regularly and maintaining them, but I stopped the insurance a couple years back. And your license … chances are it's expired."

"I didn't even think of that," Claire said.

"Anyway, we'll just pick you up tomorrow about 5:00 p.m. Then we'll take care of all the incidentals on Monday. You've got bread, cheese, and eggs for lunch."

"Thank you, Matt." Claire walked them to the door and embraced both. "I'll see you tomorrow then, Joseph."

Claire watched them drive away then closed and latched the door. She turned off the coffeepot, rinsed out the cups, and put them in the sink then wandered up to bed. She hoped sleep would overtake her, but emotions prevailed.

Soon, her pillow was wet with tears. Joe had forgiven her, had actually spoken the words: *I forgive you.* Claire didn't realize until that moment how much redemption meant to her. Her entire being ached with the need to be forgiven. If only all her sins of motherhood could be washed away by tears.

She was filled with regret and longing—longing to connect with her children and grandchildren. The thought of meeting once again with Danni and Sarah made Claire tremble with both fear and yearning.

The hours of the night passed slowly while a jet-lagged and exhausted Claire lay awake, unable to make peace with her thoughts. She longed to phone David and Iris, but it wouldn't be good to call them when she was in such an emotional state. Both of them would worry.

The last time Claire glanced at the clock it was 4:15 a.m. and her thoughts were of Sarah. Sarah would be the key. She would set the tone for what was to follow.

THE DINNER

Sarah's mixed emotions ranged from anger to anticipation. She'd spent the day cleaning and cooking, resentful of the effort she was putting forth for this dinner, yet really wanting to impress upon her mother that they were okay; no one needed her.

She was mostly upset with her girls, especially Abbie, who'd been dancing around the house all day as if it were Christmas Eve.

Sarah and Danni had decided on an Italian theme. Danni made a fabulous lasagna that Sarah asked her to bring, and she herself made a decent chicken marsala. Sarah figured that a traditional Italian dinner always included wine, and she planned to drink a lot tonight. Along with the lasagna and chicken, Sarah had roasted redskin potatoes with parsley and fresh asparagus, crusty Italian bread, and antipasto.

She'd never made tiramisu and regretted that she'd decided to try. Matt was supposed to be picking up spu-

moni and the wine but had been gone over an hour, and Sarah was wondering if he was out somewhere stomping the grapes.

At the moment, Sarah was upstairs trying to settle on an outfit for the girls.

"Abigail, it's a simple get-together, not a state dinner." Sarah groaned in exasperation. "Please explain what is wrong with your jean skirt and sweater?"

"I want to wear the blue dress!" Abbie argued. "Grandma's favorite color is blue."

Sarah, blown away by Abbie's remark, was momentarily stunned into silence. She sat on the edge of Aimee's bed and placed her head in her hands. How did she remember Grandma's favorite color? Sarah didn't even know her mother's favorite color. Abbie was only four when Mom left. Sarah was haunted by memories of the special bond Abbie and her mother had shared.

"Wear the blue dress," Sarah conceded. "But you need to pick out different shoes."

Abbie started to argue. Sarah held up a finger. She stopped.

"What about me?" Aimee whined. "If she gets to wear a dress, why can't I?"

"You can wear your pink or white dress. And wear these shoes. They'll go with either one," Sarah told her as she pulled shoes and dresses from the closet. "Uncle Joe and Christine will be here with Grandma in a half hour."

"Is Millie invited?" Aimee asked, holding up her doll.

"We don't want your stupid doll at dinner." Abbie grumped.

"Of course Millie's invited," Sarah said. "And don't you talk so rudely to your sister," she scolded Abbie. "Now get ready, both of you."

Sarah sighed and walked down the hall to her own bedroom to change. She wished she had someone standing there to tell her what to wear. She hated herself for allowing it to matter. She felt like wearing the same jeans and tee shirt she'd been cooking in all day.

Sarah kicked the bedpost. "Where in hell is my husband!" she snarled under her breath as she pulled the standard little black dress from the closet. She fixed her makeup, twisted her hair up in a clip, slipped on black pumps, and rummaged through her jewelry box for her pearl earrings from Matt.

She heard the back door opening on her way downstairs, and so did the girls.

"Grandma! Grandma!" they squealed, bounding from their room.

"It's not Grandma. It's your father!" Sarah hissed as she pointed to their room. "Do not come down until you have brushed your hair."

"Well, look at my woman." Matt smiled up at her from the bottom of the stairs.

"Don't smile at me." Sarah, hands on hips, glared down at him. "Where have you been?"

"Well, you sexy thing, I had to go to every store in the greater Chicago area to find spumoni ice cream. A couple of places thought I wanted cream for a yeast infection. By the way, have I told you how beautiful you look?"

Sarah marched down the steps and strode past him, a smile twitching at the corners of her mouth. He reached out to grab her, but she eluded his grasp and pointed upstairs. "Go change now!"

She headed for the kitchen, eyeballing the table on the way. The table looked good. Bread in the oven on warm. Chicken marsala ready. Beautiful antipasto. Dressing. Oh, dressing! Sarah looked in the refrigerator door. Half a bottle of store bought. She whipped out a carafe and mixed up olive oil, vinegar, minced garlic, water, oregano, and good old Mrs. Dash. It would do.

Matt came up behind her, wrapped his arms around her hips, and nuzzled her neck. "I don't know what smells better, you or the tiramisu."

"Bite me."

"I have every intention."

Wiping her hands on a towel, Sarah turned to face him. "I can't believe you talked me into this. Matt, you did not put on those brown corduroys!"

"What's wrong with my cords? You know I like these pants. They're comfortable."

"I laid your khakis out. And wear your loafers." She kissed him on the cheek. "Please." She pointed back upstairs.

Sarah filled the cut-glass water goblets she and Matt had gotten for their wedding and never used. *This is crazy*, she thought.

The doorbell rang as Matt was coming down the stairs. It was Danni, Rob, and the kids.

"Hey, guys." Matt kissed Danni, shook Rob's hand, and picked Lucie up. "Here's my most beautiful niece!"

Danni carried her lasagna to the kitchen and kissed Sarah on the cheek. "The table looks beautiful."

Sarah beamed and patted Danni's tummy. "Well, we have something special to celebrate."

Abbie and Aimee pranced into the kitchen and straight into Aunt Danni's waiting arms. "Look at you beautiful girls!"

"Are you excited to see Grandma too?" Aimee asked.

"Yes," Danni said. "I am. I want her to meet Lucie and Jack."

"Out to the living room, girls." Sarah commanded. "These ovens are too hot."

Rob and Matt walked in. Rob kissed Sarah.

"Beer?" Matt asked, already digging a couple out of the fridge.

"Sure," Rob answered.

"Anything we can do, babe?" Matt asked Sarah, who responded with an icy glare.

"On that note, we'll just go on out with the kids."

"How are you holding up?" Danni asked.

Sarah shrugged. "A little sorry I ever agreed to this charade, Danni. Sometimes I wish she'd never sent that letter." She poured a glass of wine and held up a toast to her sister. "I plan to drink enough for both of us."

Danni stood up and smoothed her shirt over her protruding belly. "I'm really showing."

"You look beautiful."

Danni had chosen a long, print skirt with boots and a soft, blousy peasant shirt. Her thick brown hair and eyes gave her a gypsy look. Sarah envied the bohemian look Danni had inherited from their mother.

The doorbell rang, and Sarah belted down her first glass of wine. Matt and the kids bolted for the door. Joe, Christine, and Claire walked in.

"Grandma!" Abbie fell into Claire's arms.

The lump that almost closed Claire's throat kept her from saying anything. Holding Abbie made her heart ache.

Aimee, Lucie, and Jack all stood staring, unsure whether they should jump into "Grandma's" arms.

Claire finally pushed Abbie away and held her at arm's length. "Look at how you've grown!"

Claire then hugged Aimee. "My baby. You were just a small girl when I went away." She planted a kiss on Aimee's head.

Danni stood with an arm around both her children. "Danni."

"Mom, I'd like you to meet Lucie and Jack Bradley."

Claire alternately hugged the children. "They're beautiful." Tears glistened in her eyes. She stood up and held her arms out to Danni, who hesitated, glancing back at Sarah, then stiffly embraced her mother.

Claire, overcome with emotion, dabbed at her eyes with a tissue. She hugged Rob then turned toward Sarah, who stood in the kitchen doorway. "Sarah."

"Mother." Sarah held a palm up and waved. "Nice of you to drop in."

It was Matt's turn to glare at Sarah, who ignored him. Everyone was greeting Joe and Christine. Matt grabbed a beer for Joe, and Christine headed to the kitchen, following Sarah. Claire was being dragged upstairs. "Come and see our room, Grandma!" All the kids followed.

Christine looked beautiful and richly appointed in a cashmere sweater and wool skirt. Her long, white-blond hair hung smoothly over her shoulders. A Prada bag and shoes completed her ensemble.

"I wish you'd teach me how to dress," said Sarah. "Wine?"

"Yes to the wine," Christine replied. "And you're wearing the basic black dress. How much more perfect

162

can you get? Besides, your mother is wearing almost the exact dress. And she's absolutely beautiful."

Sarah glared. "Danni, pour Christine a glass of wine and refill my glass."

Danni complied. "How was the drive over?" Danni asked Christine.

"Your mother is charming." Christine sipped her wine. "Although she is worried about how the two of you will receive her."

Sarah belted down a second glass of wine. "Oh, yeah?" Danni said nothing. "We should sit down to dinner while everything is hot," Sarah said.

Christine went to round the family up. Sarah guided people to their seats. She placed her mother far away from herself. Brutus and Clementine both showed up at the dinner table. "Out!" Matt yelled, pointing toward the doorway.

"My word, is that Clementine?" Claire looked shocked.

"Yes," Sarah answered. "Did you think I could leave her alone at the house for four years?"

Everyone fell silent. "Joe, would you say the blessing?" Matt asked.

Joe stood and cleared his throat. Sarah and Danni hushed the children, and the table quieted. Joe started with the standard Catholic prayer then asked for God's blessing to keep the family safe. He continued, "I am grateful that we are here all together as a family again."

Sarah fidgeted with her silverware. Matt placed his hand over hers.

"I know that the last four and a half years have been difficult ones for all of us. I don't know how I would have made it without Matt and Sarah. But I know now that

Mom had some difficult times too. And I hope we can work toward healing this family. And last, I am thankful to have two sisters who are great cooks."

Everyone chuckled. Claire's tears flowed freely down her cheeks. Abbie leaned toward her and laid her head on her arm.

The table was large enough to comfortably seat twelve people, and Sarah's decorations were simple and elegant. Everyone complimented Sarah on how wonderful all the food tasted. She reminded them that they were dining on Danni's famous lasagna.

Claire helped the little ones with their plates. Danni was pleased that they seemed to take right to her. There was small talk throughout the meal.

Near the end of the dinner, Joe stood up once again. "I'd like to propose a toast." Everyone quieted. "First of all, I'd of course like to thank Sarah and Matt for hosting this wonderful dinner." He placed his hand on Danni's shoulder. "And Danni, of course, for the best lasagna this side of Italy." He sighed and continued. "I also have some happy news to share." He reached out for Christine's hand. "Christine and I are getting married."

For the first time that day, Sarah really smiled. Everyone cheered and clapped and left their seats to hug and kiss the couple. Christine showed off a large solitaire. The girls oohed and aahed. Abbie was mesmerized by the large stone.

Glasses clinked around the table, wishing the couple all the best.

"It's about time you roped her in!" exclaimed Matt, who patted Joe on the back then hugged him. "We can use a good tax attorney in this family, especially after

you cooked the books at the dental office on your summer breaks."

Everyone laughed.

"Will you be our aunt Christine?" asked Aimee.

"Yes." Christine smiled. "And I would like all of you to be in our wedding."

"All of us!" exclaimed Abbie.

"Yes, you and Aimee and Lucie and Jack."

Aimee beamed. Abbie looked as though she would burst from bliss. Christine leaned in toward Sarah and Danni. "I've asked my sister, Pauline, to be my maid of honor, and I'd like both of you to stand up with us."

"Yes." Danni smiled. Sarah nodded. "I'm so happy for Joe." She patted Christine's hand. "I prayed he would find someone to love and share his life."

"Do we get to pick out our dresses?" asked Abbie.

"Abigail!" Sarah scolded. "Don't be so rude!"

Christine laughed. "How about if we pick them out together? Won't it be fun to shop for them?" She turned toward Claire. "Claire, I hope you'll be here for the wedding." Claire smiled.

Rob stood up and asked for everyone's attention. Surprised, Danni sat back, wondering what her normally quiet husband had to say.

"I wanted to say how happy I am that Christine will finally be moving up in line from *W* to *B*, which is why I suspect she's really marrying this guy."

Everyone around the table laughed.

"That's exactly why I said yes!" Christine patted Joe's back.

"And we also have an announcement to make," continued Rob. "Danni and I are expecting number three."

Danni looked stunned. Once again, the table came alive with congratulations and hugs.

"How did you know?" a shocked Danni whispered to her husband.

"My wife shuns coffee in the morning and pulls the saltines out of the cupboard; I get the hint. And I couldn't be happier."

It was Danni's turn to cry. Rob embraced her and chided her for not telling him sooner, for not sharing her doubts and fears.

"I was afraid you'd be disappointed with me," Danni whispered.

Rob lifted her chin with his finger and kissed her forehead. "I could never be disappointed with you."

Sarah smiled. The dinner had had a purpose after all. Mom was seeing everything she'd missed out on.

Matt brought out a second bottle of wine as Sarah served the tiramisu, spumoni, and coffee. The kids were tired of sitting and were excused after they wolfed down their dessert.

"Go put in a movie in the den," Sarah told Abbie.

"Come with us, Grandma." Abbie pulled her hand.

"I want to talk with the adults for a little while; then I'll come join you."

"Go on," Matt commanded.

Sarah stood up. "Well, I'm going to start clearing up."

"Please, Sarah." Claire looked to her daughter. "Sit for a few minutes. Please."

Sarah reluctantly sat back down. The table was hushed and waited for Claire to start.

"It's difficult to explain four and a half years." Claire's voice cracked. "And I'm not really sure where to start."

She looked to Danni and Sarah. "I just don't know how to start, but there are things I need to tell you."

"Mom"—Joe took her hand—"just tell them. Like you told us." He gestured to Matt. Sarah stared at Matt intently.

"Oh"—Claire shook her head—"there's so much more to tell. As you know, I've been in England."

CLAIRE'S STORY

Claire had very little memory of the flight overseas— only standing on foreign soil with nowhere to go.

She'd never felt so alone and lost. She stood in the airport, passport in hand, agonizing over all that was behind her. Claire felt that her survival hinged on her ability to run away from everyone and everything familiar to her.

The family she loved would want and need things she was unable to provide. And Jack was no longer there to guide her, to tell her what needed to be done. Claire was lost.

Cold and sick and frightened, she had wandered outside and asked a cabbie to take her to a hotel. The cabbie stared at her then sped away, dropping her a short time later at the Brook's Inn, a run-down, old brownstone. Claire paid him and stood on the sidewalk in the dim light, wondering for the first time if she'd brought enough money with her.

She had cleared out her checking account and carried a little over three thousand dollars in her purse.

A Sikh sat behind the counter and stared at Claire as she timidly walked in with her two suitcases. She queried about weekly or monthly rates.

The Sikh gave her a price, but Claire knew nothing about pounds conversion and blinked. "In American dollars?"

With her cash reserves, Claire paid for one month up front without even asking to see the room. No questions were asked.

After registering, she was escorted up the narrow stairs to her room. The Sikh neither offered to carry her suitcases nor waited for her approval of the room before he handed her the key and walked away.

"Lavatory?" she called after him.

He pointed toward the end of the hall.

The small studio provided a pull-down bed, linens, a hot plate, and a small sink. She shared a bath with other residents on the floor. Claire sat upon the creaky bed with its threadbare covers and wept. She stayed in her room for a day and a half before she ventured out, hunger driving an urge to move.

She looked for a grocer, thinking she would just buy something and take it back to her dark room. Claire stayed weeks in the room, often lying awake in the dark, listening to the sounds of the night and longing for her mind to find some kind of peace.

Eventually, the room seemed to close in on her, and Claire began to venture out. Frightened and lonely, Claire sunk deeper into despair. During the day she walked the streets of London, fearful of anyone who glanced her way. She ate very little, took scant notice of her appearance, and once became lost and could not find her way back to the rooming house.

Afraid to ask anyone directions, Claire ambled along, clinging her pocketbook tightly against her chest. Pedestrians that passed by her stared at her as if she were a madwoman. It was dark when Claire finally stumbled upon the rooming house.

Her throat constricted tightly as she stifled a sob and fell upon her bed. She felt feverish and sick. When she cried into her pillow and whispered, "I'd be better off dead," she felt an overwhelming sense of relief. Once the thought had entered Claire's mind, she began to feel better and could make a plan of action.

I am dead inside already, she thought. With a calm purpose, Claire took family photos from her pocketbook, taking care not to look at them. She continued to empty her purse until every reminder of who she was had been removed. She placed the cash she had left on the bed for whoever would find it, placed her purse items in the dingy sink, and held matches to them until they started to burn.

She stared down at the family photos, curling and melting away, her driver's license, checkbook, passport. Then she calmly picked out a plastic razor from her toiletries bag and broke it open with her shoe.

Now that she had made a decision to do something, Claire felt better. The thin razor blade she removed from the broken razor seemed sharp enough to do the job.

Claire sat down to think about the best way to do it. She decided that waiting until the middle of the night would be best so other residents wouldn't need the bathroom as much. Claire sighed, looked down at the cash

on the bed, and decided she would like a drink. It would make things easier.

She walked across the street, cash in hand and paid for a bottle of scotch. Claire had only tasted scotch once in her life and had hated it. Now she would make herself drink it; it would be her medicine.

Back in her room, Claire sat on the bed, sipping her scotch from a filmy glass. She felt nauseous but determined and made herself drink enough until she felt numb and woozy.

She lay on the bed, her wristwatch in hand, sipping the scotch and watching the time. She allowed her mind thoughts of Jack, of the wasted years he had spent with others, and wept.

Finally, at 4:00 a.m., Claire made her way to the bathroom, carrying the razor blade wrapped in a towel and her bottle of scotch. She knocked before entering and stared down at the grimy tub. She took another swallow of the scotch then started undressing.

She gave no thought to the fact that she would be naked when people found her. She only felt relief that her pain would soon be gone. And the thought of that provided the impetus for Claire to seek the release of death.

Sinking down in the warmth of the tub, she took deep breaths and willed herself to relax. She prayed for only one thing: to have enough courage to complete the deed.

The stinging pain of the razor shocked her momentarily. She stared down at the water turning pink. She traced the razor across the other wrist with a sharp intake of breath then leaned against the back of the tub.

THE LONG SLEEP

A Pakistani woman had been pounding on the restroom door long enough to wake most of the other residents of the floor. A crowd gathered outside the bathroom door.

"Maybe no one's in there. Maybe it just locked on its own."

The Sikh was summoned from downstairs and arrived with a key, and a crowd of Claire's neighbors converged in the bathroom to witness a sight many of them wished they hadn't seen.

The London police and medical services were summoned. The Sikh checked for a pulse and nodded to the others. "She's still alive."

The ambulance siren shrieked through the city as it motored toward the nearest hospital. The doctors and nurses worked frantically to save the poor woman who had tried so hard to die.

The police were full of questions about the woman. The Sikh was certain she was American. Her room revealed little; she'd burned her IDs. But the passport had not succumbed completely to the small sink fire, and Claire's name and part of her photo remained intact.

Claire hadn't thought of the registration she'd so diligently filled out many weeks ago. The policemen bagged the passport and other items and took down sketchy information from the neighbors and the Sikh.

While the police investigated, Claire was admitted to the hospital emergency room as a Jane Doe. The next few days were touch and go for Claire, but in the end it was determined that Claire would live.

The policemen came to the hospital to check on her condition, to put a number to the face, to update their records. Interpol had nothing on the woman; she was not listed as a missing person.

The physicians were unable to elicit any response from her. She had shut down mentally. She was aphasic and catatonic. They found no response to painful stimuli or gentle caresses. Claire was no longer Claire.

A call was placed to Bethlem Royal regarding the transfer of a failed suicide victim, previously identified as a homeless Jane Doe and now identified as an American, Claire Bradley, in a catatonic state.

She had been admitted, they reported, with alcohol poisoning and blood loss one-third.

Claire was subjected to a battery of testing for substance abuse, metabolic disorders, toxins, and brain anomalies.

When outside influences were ruled out, Claire was started on a regimen of drugs and became a total care patient.

She received daily occupational and physical therapy and stimulation designed to wake up her sleeping brain.

Months passed without a response, until the nurse on duty found Claire on the floor one night. "She's moved on her own," the nurse reported.

"Is she responsive?"

"No different, no. It's just that I found her on the floor."

"Use soft restraints," the physician ordered. "Maybe our American lady is finally waking up."

Claire had undergone one ECT without success; now the physician thought it was time to try again.

Electro convulsive therapy, although barbaric to some people's minds, had re-emerged in the field of psychiatry and was having success in many difficult cases of severe depression. Claire's psychiatrist was sure that a severe depression had driven Claire to attempt suicide. ECT was much more humane in today's practice, with the use of sedation.

ECT for Claire, however, remained unsuccessful. She underwent three separate treatments. Nothing changed for Claire except for voluntary movement and response to painful stimuli. The staff continued to use restraints for her safety and tried to reach her mind.

THE AWAKENING

The first conscious memory Claire had of the sanitarium was awakening to institutional gray green walls—of trepidation, creeping cold, and discomfort.

In a fog and drugged haze, she remembered frightening feelings of uneasiness. She knew nothing about herself, her past. Her arms and legs felt heavy and numb. She blinked, noticing that her eyes were dry and sore.

Her heart was thudding in her chest and temples; Claire made her breathing slow and tried to make her brain work. She was disjointed. Her arms and legs would not work. She could not lift her head.

Claire slowly realized that her wrists were tied with cotton bindings to the bed rails. Willing herself to move her feet, she realized that they too were bound.

Claire felt chilled and shook from fear and shock. *Who am I?* She started to perspire profusely. She tried to cry out. "Aaagh." Her throat was dry and constricted. She was unaware that a feeding tube snaked through her nose,

making her throat sore. She tried to lick her lips but felt no moisture there. Her tongue was swollen, cracked, and dry and involuntarily darted in and out of her mouth.

She heard the door latch click and watched as it swung open. Heart pounding, she watched two women enter the room, one thick, one thin. They both stopped in their tracks when they saw Claire staring at them.

"My Lord, the highness is awake." The thick one stared at Claire briefly then approached the bed. "She's mussed herself again." She clucked her tongue at Claire. "Now that you're back to the land of the living, perhaps you'll be able to control your bodily functions and save us all some work."

"Gracie,"—she gestured—"get us some clean nappies and a cover-up for her highness."

The matronly woman filled a basin with sudsy water, removed the adult diaper from Claire, and proceeded to wash her bottom. The shock of the cold water caused her teeth to clack together.

"Yes, dear. It's cold, but the pipes here don't give us warm water half the time. You'll get used to being cold. It's never bothered you before. It's kind of nice to know you're feeling the cold. My name is Margaret, by the way. Gracie and I have been taking care of you for some time. It's nice to finally meet you, Claire."

The matron worked efficiently and talked softly to Claire all the time she worked on her. Gracie arrived with fresh linens, and together they made up the bed with Claire still in it. They put a fresh cover gown atop her, tying it around her neck.

"Gracie, fetch us a pitcher of water for her highness and some glasses. We'll have a toast to the living."

The matron held Claire's head up and placed a straw to her lips. She wasn't sure what to do with the straw. The matron massaged her throat, and slowly Claire sucked a small bit of water into her mouth. She immediately choked and coughed.

"You're okay, dear. You've pretty much been asleep for several months. Your muscles don't know how to work. The medication you've been on causes your tongue to swell."

Claire stared. She was trying to compute the information she'd just been given. She tried to make her voice work, but she was unable to form a word. Her mind was imploding, but she was unable to move or communicate.

The young nurse placed a hand on her forehead and alternately held her eyes open and squeezed ointment into them. Everything was blurry.

She felt their hands on her body, massaging her arms and legs, listening to her heart and lungs, placing a thermometer under her tongue. Unaware that she had an IV through a central line, Claire wondered what was happening when she felt a burning sensation up her arm, and then she was gone.

"Poor thing." Gracie shook her head. "She looked a fright."

"Now, Gracie. You've been here long enough to know not to let your heart go out. She's had enough shock treatments and meds to kill a horse, and yet she survived all we've done to her, hasn't she? She's a strong one, her highness is."

The matron patted the young girl's arm. "You watch her close now. I'm going to call Dr. Diebel with the news."

The following weeks for Claire were filled with misery and pain. They removed the feeding tube and slowly introduced pureed food. She had to learn to swallow liquid and pureed food first, then to chew. The IV was weaned and swallowing became easier, and Claire was placed on oral medications.

They slowly got her up out of bed, first to a chair and then to ambulate. Weakened muscles cried out in agony. Claire would sob and struggle, but she was no match for her caretakers anymore. She had become a skeletal waif.

They kept a leather belt about her waist that they used as a handhold; then she was tied to the chair with a posey belt or tied to the bed. But Claire was really a prisoner in her mind. Her thoughts, like her body, were disjointed. She would have brief periods of lucidity, and her caregivers would try to make her speak, but Claire kept her jaw clenched to keep her tongue inside.

She had endured much since her failed suicide attempt and had no memory of the act itself and no memory of her past. The only thing she felt she had left was her will. As much as her captors cajoled her to talk, she would not speak or try to communicate.

She was a prisoner to their whims and their will, but she would not allow them into her private world.

At night she lay tormented; demons plagued her thoughts. *Demons from what? What have I done? Who am I?* As much as Claire wanted answers, she feared the answers most; she controlled her desire for knowledge.

They had long since stopped tying her to the bed or chair. Her muscle tone had improved, along with her balance. Claire was given limited freedom. Although still locked in her room at night, she was allowed to wander the halls, was expected to take her meals with the other

residents in the dining room, and for several hours a day was sent to the common room.

She shrunk away from the others—those frightful, mad creatures with haunted eyes who stumbled about on unsteady feet. She often sat near the window and stared with wonder at the outdoors.

Dr. Diebel was stymied at her lack of progress. He silently stared at Claire during their weekly sessions, trying to determine the best course of action. "Claire, why won't you talk to me? You realize that we know who you are? You're an American citizen. Your name is Claire Bradley."

The police, after establishing Claire's identity and country and finding no interest in the woman by Interpol, had discontinued their investigation and found nothing more out about Claire.

"Claire, can you explain how you ended up in England? Do you have family?"

Claire stared out the window, oblivious to Dr. Diebel.

He sighed and looked at his schedule to see if he had an opening for ECT. He worried that another ECT might cause irreparable damage. Dr. Diebel drummed his fingers on the desk.

"Claire, I'm considering another ECT session for you. How can we ever get you home if you won't communicate with us?"

The word *home* had sent a jolt through Claire. This was home, the only existence she knew.

Dr. Diebel noticed the change in her demeanor. He suspected that Claire understood him but was not responding for whatever reason. What had happened to this poor woman? "Claire, you've been with us for nine months. I know that you can speak."

The session ended as it always did—unproductive. Dr. Diebel's heart was heavy. If they didn't find the key to unlock the door to this woman's psyche soon, she might be lost to them forever.

He picked up his phone and called a friend. "Iris, I'm calling to request your assistance on a case."

Thus began a relationship that finally broke the bonds of madness for Claire. Iris Neville, an academic and a psychologist, took over Claire's difficult case. She made twice-weekly visits to Bethlem.

Instead of sessions, Iris referred to their hours as "walks." With Dr. Diebel's blessing, Iris and Claire strolled the grounds of Bethlem.

Like a child, Claire's face was easy to read and revealed signs of wonder and joy at the outdoors. For weeks, their conversations were one sided—Iris chattering on about her classes, her garden, her favorite wine. Claire at times seemed oblivious to her companion, but other times Iris sensed a change in Claire, that she might be listening.

A breakthrough came when Iris became ill with pneumonia. She missed an entire month of visits. No one bothered to explain this to Claire. They just escorted her to weekly sessions with Dr. Diebel. Claire retreated farther into herself. Dr. Diebel scheduled another ECT session for her the following week.

"Please, Herman, don't do it," Iris pleaded from her hospital bed. "I truly believe that Claire's mind was coming back." Iris reached for him. "Please, Herman, hold off. I beg you."

Dr. Diebel patted his dear friend's hand. "Very well. For you."

Iris returned to Claire after five weeks. It was coming up close to one year since Claire had been admitted to Bethlem. When she first saw her, Claire's heart thudded in her chest and her cheeks flushed. She didn't understand her feelings of anger and abandonment and joy.

"I've missed you." Iris smiled. Claire turned her back to her. "Now, now. It's all right, Claire. I've been ill, but I'm better. Just like you've been ill and you're getting better."

Iris had never touched Claire, but now she approached her and placed a hand on her shoulder.

Claire stiffened, too frightened to move. Iris just stood silently, her hand resting on Claire's shoulder.

"Claire, won't you walk with me? The apples should be ready to pick. Take my hand. Won't you, Claire?"

Claire turned, looked at Iris's face. "You left me."

Iris did her best not to show shock or reveal the tremendous joy she felt.

"I'm back now." Iris held out her hand. Claire slipped her tiny, bony hand into Iris's gnarled, old one. They walked the grounds together and sat and ate an apple on the grass. Claire said nothing more.

That was okay with Iris, and she didn't push. Claire had given her a reason to keep coming back, a reason to hope for Claire.

Iris increased their sessions to three, sometimes four a week. Claire fatigued easily and would complain when Iris badgered her.

Slowly, just as it was in that other lifetime, Claire came back little by little. Broken pieces of memories came back. She remembered her home and Jack. One sunny after-

noon as Claire waited and watched for Iris in the common room, one of the matrons was calling a patient across the room. "Sarah! Sarah!"

Claire, shocked and numb, fell to her knees and rocked back and forth, her head in her hands.

"Iris, I have children," she poured out to her friend when she arrived. The memories now seemed to flood every conscious thought she had every hour of the day and became too much for Claire. She retreated to her shell, begging Iris to push no more.

"I don't want to know!" she cried.

"You must confront your demons, Claire," Iris persisted. "Trust me. You'll see."

"What happened to me?" Claire sat on the grass; a tear slipped down her cheek. "What did I do?" She placed her head down on her knees, and her voice was soft, muffled. "I've sinned against my family. Against my God. I wish I had died."

"Don't ever say that," Iris admonished her. "Sins come in all shades, Claire, and our lives are colored with them. You must find forgiveness in yourself. You must find some peace." Iris smoothed her hair back and lifted her chin. "Perhaps, if you would allow me to contact your family—"

"No! Swear to me, Iris. Swear! I can never face them again. Ever. Promise me."

"I won't go against your wishes, but, Claire, you must understand that you'll never be whole again until you confront your past."

The next few weeks, Claire progressed rapidly. Iris worried about her health; she was so underweight, a waif

of a girl. The sanitarium didn't have mirrors, and Claire had no idea what she looked like.

Iris placed a compact mirror in her hand, and Claire was shocked at what stared back at her—one of those frightful, mad creatures with wild eyes that she'd been so fearful of in the common room.

"I'm going to request a day pass for you. We'll have a salon day."

Claire looked frightened. "No. I don't want to leave."

"Claire, this is not your home. You're getting well, and our goal is to get you back to the outside world. Dr. Diebel is a friend of mine. I think I can negotiate a day trip from him."

Iris would not take no for an answer. She took Claire to a salon and treated her to a coloring, plus a cut, style, manicure, and facial. Claire's hair had turned mostly white, and the stylist colored it to her beautiful, shiny dark brown again. After the facial, the beautician applied makeup. Claire looked at herself in the mirror and felt that her past was now part of her present.

Iris then took her to her dentist. Claire had lost a front tooth during one of the ECT sessions, and her teeth—from poor nutrition, the medicines, and neglect—were in desperate need of attention.

The dentist made several appointments for repairs, caps, and bleaching.

"I can't pay!" Claire wailed.

"I intend to have you pay me back when you get a decent job, young lady!"

Claire was pleased and excited. She spent several sessions talking with Dr. Diebel, who was amazed at the

progress Iris had made with her. He immediately started working toward her release.

Claire was finally discharged on December 19, one long year after she was admitted. She left the grounds of Bethlem in a new pantsuit from Iris and with a card filled with money collected from the staff.

They had surprised her with a small farewell cake and a good-luck card with almost two hundred pounds they'd collected. Claire was overwhelmed.

She was taken to a halfway residents' house where she was assigned her own room and chores.

Iris clucked her tongue. "It's just a stopping point, dear. I've arranged a job interview for you at the bookstore I send my students to. He owes me a favor. After you've saved a little money, we'll look for a flat."

Together they used some of the money to buy a few outfits and necessities. Claire threw herself into her new life, her job, and her weekly therapy sessions with Iris. She remained on the antidepressants. She saved every penny she could, sometimes lingering outside the coffee shop so she could just smell the warm rolls and coffee.

Iris surprised her one day and drove her to a charming little apartment over an old building within walking distance of her job. "I know it needs some fresh paint and a good cleaning, but I've paid the security deposit and the first and last months' rent. It's yours."

Claire wept. "Oh, Iris. I can never repay you. Never."

Together, like the closest of friends, they shopped at thrift stores and antiques shops. Iris was unable to paint because of her arthritis, but she supervised Claire's work and voiced her opinions about her color choices.

Claire, for the first time in her life, felt independent. She was still plagued with guilt and grieved over the loss of her children, but a secure happiness was creeping into the corners of her mind for the first time since she could remember.

She opened up about her past in her therapy sessions. Being a child bride. Her married life with Jack. Living with his infidelities.

Claire was purged and cleansed.

A TALE'S END

Everyone sat in silence as Claire recited her story. She attempted to be truthful without being too graphic or emotional.

Danni wept at times; Claire leaned over the table to squeeze her hand. Christine looked sympathetically back and forth between Claire and Joe, who stared at the tablecloth. Matt and Rob both did their share of staring at their plates.

Sarah stared out the window and turned her fork over and over as she listened. Tines up, tines down.

"So," Claire concluded, "I realized that I wanted to reconnect with all of you, to ask your forgiveness and to explain."

Her voice cracked under the strain. "*Sorry* seems like such an empty word. How does one apologize for such a cowardly act?"

"Oh, Mom," Danni cried. "We forgive you. We've all made mistakes. You're back now. That's all that counts."

Rob wrapped his arms around her shaking shoulders. Claire placed her head in her hands, elbows propped on the table. It was done.

"Mom." Joe took her hand. "Mom." She looked up at the son she had deserted. "We can rebuild our family. We all want that." He gestured around the table. "You still have family here."

"Well." Sarah placed her palms down on the table and stood up. "I'm going to clean up."

Matt stared at his wife, who dropped her napkin and turned her back on the table. He waited until she was out of earshot then patted Claire's hand. "Don't take it too hard, Claire. Sarah's a good girl." He shrugged. "She needs some time."

Christine and Danni excused themselves and carried plates to the kitchen. Claire could hear Danni and Sarah having words.

"Matt," Claire asked, "would you mind taking me home if I want to stay a while?"

"Sure." He nodded.

"Maybe you should come with Christine and me," Joe pressed.

"No." Claire was adamant. "I need to talk with Sarah and Matt."

Claire made her way to the den and curled up on the sofa with the children. Sarah caught glimpses of them on her way back and forth from the dining room to the kitchen; Jack on her lap, Lucie, Abbie, and Aimee curled up with her, the dog and cat at her feet. "Unbelievable," she muttered. "It's like she never left."

The guys drank a few beers and shot some pool for the next hour. Then Rob checked his watch. "Well, it's

been great, but I'm going to get Danni moving. The kids need to go to bed."

Everyone said their good-byes at the front door, and Sarah gave Danni an extra-long hug. "Call me," she said. She kissed Lucie, Jack, and Rob. "Make her get some rest," she ordered Rob.

"I will."

Sarah hugged Christine and Joe. "I'm happy. So happy for you both."

"Thanks." Christine smiled. "I'll be in touch. Your dinner was wonderful."

"Sarah." Joe leaned in. "Take it easy on her."

Matt walked everyone out to their cars. Sarah pointed up the stairs and ordered the girls to bed. "It's late. It's past your bedtime."

"But Grandma's here."

Sarah clenched her jaw.

"How about if I tuck you in?" asked Claire, looking at Sarah. "Would that be okay, Sarah?"

"Sure." She marched off to the kitchen. Matt locked the front door and came in to help.

"You came off a little cold," he offered.

"Don't start, Matt. I'm not in the mood."

"Dinner was great."

Sarah practically tossed the dishes into the dishwasher. Matt was concerned that he had allowed Claire to stay. Sarah's anger was boiling under the surface. He was worried she would say something that would cause irreparable damage to the relationship that would affect all of them.

"Chill, Sarah."

"You know, I'm sick and tired, Matt. I'm sick of hearing it from Danni, and I'm sick of hearing it from Joe, and I'm sick and tired of hearing it from you. I'm trying to protect everyone here, and I'm the only one who knows it."

"Is it the control, Sarah? Is that it? I know you're just like your dad, and God forbid he ever lost the control. You've been the one to orchestrate all of our lives, and now with your mom back in the picture, you might have to give up some of that control."

"Go to hell, Matt!" Sarah spat at him. She sat at the table and broke down in tears. Matt sat down next to her and reached for her hand, but she pulled it away.

"Sarah," Matt whispered. "Where is all this anger coming from? What's happening here?"

He looked up to see Claire leaning on the doorjamb. "They're in bed."

"Are you ready to go home?" Matt asked hopefully.

Claire looked at Sarah with concern. "I hoped we could talk some more Sarah."

Sarah got up from the table and wiped her eyes. "I'm kind of all talked out." She slammed the dishwasher door. "Kind of tired."

"Sarah." Claire sat at the kitchen table. "I realize how angry you are. I know I left the mess for you. I know what a financial burden you and Matthew assumed. I want a chance to make it right. That's all."

Sarah turned and faced her. "You don't know how angry I am. You have no idea. I feel you don't know me at all. I certainly don't know you."

"If my accounts are intact, I can pay you both back. I just want you to give me a chance, Sarah. I do know you. I knew that you would be the hardest of all. And you do

know me. I'm exactly everything you're thinking—weak, cowardly. But I'm trying, and I want you to give me a chance. That's all I want. A chance."

"You want a hell of a lot more from me than that. And it just isn't in me." Sarah started to walk from the room. "I'm going to bed."

"Sarah," Claire called out. "I'd like to take the girls to England. I've missed them so much."

Sarah had frozen in her tracks and turned suddenly. "How dare you!" she screamed. She turned on Claire like a protective lioness. Claire cringed. "How dare you ask such a thing! How dare you say you've missed them! I would never allow you to take my children anywhere. You might abandon them somewhere when you're tired of playing grandmother."

Claire stood up. "You can hate me, but your daughters do not hate me. They can find forgiveness in their hearts, Sarah. I never stopped loving any of you."

Sarah's shoulders slumped. "I'll never understand your kind of love, Mother. You're right. Abbie and Aimee are glad you're here. And I'm going to be very generous and allow you to see them because it's what they want. But it will be under my terms." She pointed her finger at Claire. "I won't have them hurt again."

"I promise I won't hurt them." Claire looked beseechingly at her daughter. "I'm so sorry for the hurt I've caused you, Sarah. I may never be able to convince you, but I love you."

Sarah turned and walked upstairs.

Matt drove Claire home in silence. She didn't speak until they turned in the drive. "I'll never make it right with her." She shook her head.

"It was just too much too soon." Matt patted her hand. He got out of the car and walked his mother-in-law to the door.

"What's the answer, Matt?"

"I wish I knew, Claire. Just take a day at a time." He kissed her cheek. "I'll call you Monday around noon, and we'll get some of your running taken care of."

Matt felt drained when he climbed the stairs to bed. Sarah lay with her back to him. He brushed his teeth, climbed into bed, and sensed her stiffen when he pressed up against her back.

He could feel her anger generated toward him now. "I'm tired, Matt."

"Me too," he agreed, rolling over, too exhausted to argue.

TOUCH MY HEART

Claire lay in bed, propped up on pillows, phone in hand. She needed to make calls to David and Iris. As she debated about whom to call first, her phone rang in her hand.

"David."

"Hey, I've been worried about you. You know how to leave a chap on pins and needles."

Claire smiled. "You must have been reading my thoughts. I actually was holding the phone to dial you up."

"I miss you. How's it going?"

"About how I expected. No, wait...better than I expected. Two of my children have forgiven me. Actually spoke the words. And my beautiful grandchildren...oh, David, you should see."

"I wanted to come. I should have come. But someone wouldn't let me." David groaned. "Oh, Claire. How did I let you go?"

"I miss you too," Claire whispered. "Being here"—she paused—"it doesn't feel like me anymore. This place. It doesn't feel like home anymore. England feels like home. You're my home."

"I needed to hear that. When are you coming back?"

"There are so many things going on. My son is getting married. Danni is expecting number three." She paused. "Sarah is being difficult. I knew she would be." Claire sighed. "David, I have to stay for a while. I owe them all that."

"I could still come."

"Not yet. I need time. Please, David. You have to trust me. I do want you to meet my family, but I need more time."

"Claire."

"I miss you as much as you miss me."

Claire held the phone against her chest after they hung up, as if David was still there. She then dialed Iris.

"Hello."

"Iris, it's Claire."

"Thank God. Claire, I've worried about you."

"I'm all right."

Hearing Iris's voice made Claire cry. She stifled a sob with her fist as tears streaked down her cheeks. How could one person hold so many tears? Claire's heart felt as heavy as a rock.

Iris sat silent.

"It's good to hear your voice," Claire spoke softly. "It's been a difficult couple of days."

"Did they see you?"

"Yes. Joseph and Matthew picked me up at the airport. I had dinner with all of my family tonight. At Sarah

and Matt's." Claire's voice cracked. "I saw all of my grand-children, Iris."

"And are they willing to re-establish some kind of relationship with you?"

Claire shrugged as if Iris could see her. "Joseph and Danni welcomed me back. Sarah, of course, is the difficult one. I knew that she would be. We're very different. She's a lot like Jack."

"Yes, I know." Iris had heard all of this before. "Claire, I encouraged … no, I urged you to go back and face your family. But I'm worried by the way you sound."

"No, you're wrong. I am strong enough. I just need more time. I can do this, Iris."

"Please be careful, Claire."

Claire and Iris said their good-byes, and Claire washed her face and brushed her teeth.

Her body was tired and her mind exhausted. "God please," she prayed, "let me sleep tonight."

The last thing she remembered before drifting off to sleep was checking the alarm clock. Danni was picking her up in the morning for mass, and Claire intended to be ready on time.

DANNI

TIME TO REUNITE

"Are you sure it's okay for me to stay home?" Rob asked just before he went to sleep.

Danni curled up next to him. "Yes. It will give Mom and me a chance to talk. You've been working six days a week for months without a day off. You can sleep in, be lazy."

Her philosophy didn't work, though. Rob was up with her and the kids, helping get them dressed for church while Danni fought the nausea that hit as soon as she was upright.

"Why do we have to go to church if Daddy doesn't?" whined Lucie.

"Both your grandmas will be there."

"Both?"

"Yes," Rob told her. "And you need to behave. I don't want to hear from your mother that you didn't sit still in

mass. After church, you and Jack are going to Grandma and Papa's house so that Mom can visit with Grandma Claire."

Danni and Claire walked into church side by side, Claire holding Jack in her arms. They slid into the pew next to Elena and Pedro.

Elena and Pedro leaned toward Claire and embraced her and patted her hand. Both children were delighted to see their familiar grandparents who welcomed them onto their laps.

Danni thanked God in her prayers to have her mother back. She needed her mother. It would take some time for the children to warm up to her, but Danni felt confident it would happen. After church, Elena and Pedro bundled Lucie and Jack in their car. Danni and Claire stood on the sidewalk and waved good-bye.

"They have car seats?"

"Of course," Danni said. "They have lots of grand-children, and they are always with them."

"They're good people."

"Yes. I'm very lucky. Sarah frequently reminds me of that." Danni smiled. "Where would you like to eat lunch?"

"Is the deli still there?"

"Yes."

"I would love a turkey Reuben and a good helping of potato salad."

They settled in a booth at the deli, Claire with coffee and Danni with water.

"I feel so good, Mom. I can't believe we're sitting here. Dad always loved this place."

Claire stared at the table.

"I'm sorry, Mom. I shouldn't bring Dad up, I suppose."

"No, Danni. No." Claire took her hand. "It's fine for you to bring up your father. Sometimes it just overwhelms me how many memories are flooding back. Your father played such a large part in all of our lives."

"He did." Danni smiled. She looked ten years old again. "Do you remember how much he hated Rob when I brought him home?"

Claire nodded, smiling.

"And when I said I was going to drop out of school and get married; why, I'm not sure why that didn't just kill him dead right then!" Danni chuckled. "And Matt saved the day. He popped a couple beers, calmed Dad down, and said, 'Just think of it this way, Jack; you're not losing a daughter, you're gaining a car mechanic!'"

They laughed together, and Claire thought how wonderful it felt to laugh with her daughter.

"Do you still miss him, Mom?"

Claire smiled. "Yes, I miss him. I always felt taken care of when your father was alive."

Danni nodded. "I think we all did."

"But I'm with someone else now." Claire stared at the table and picked at her fingers, a small smile playing at the corners of her mouth.

"Tell me about him!" Danni whispered, leaning in close. Danni had already seen his picture, the grainy photo Sarah received from the private detective agency. But she didn't think Claire knew about that.

"His name is David. David Frost. Very English. And he's young. He's twelve years younger than me."

Claire looked into Danni's face, trying to read any disapproval. Danni only smiled.

"But you look amazing, Mom. You could pass for someone fifteen years younger."

Claire laughed.

"He's amazing. I tried to dissuade him, but he was so persistent. He'd come into the bookstore every day and tell me I had to go out with him to save him from becoming one of those stalkers." She glowed as she spoke of him. "He's got that English sense of humor." She shrugged.

"Oh, Mom. You seem so happy." Danni suddenly seemed sad. "I'm afraid you're going to leave again."

Claire leaned back in her seat. "Danni, I am going back to England. It's my home now."

Danni looked stricken.

"But," Claire continued, "I want all of us to have a real relationship again, and we all need to visit back and forth." Claire could see Danni's crestfallen appearance and talked faster. "I plan to visit regularly, and I want all of you to visit me."

Now it was Danni's turn to slouch down in her seat, tears welling in her eyes. "Mom, I was hoping you'd be here for this baby." She looked up. "Don't get me wrong. I'm happy for you, but Rob and I won't ever see England; that's for sure."

"Danni, I will be here for this one. I know I've let you down before. I plan to take a vacation when you're due. Maybe David will come too." Claire patted Danni's hand. "Please, Danni. Tell me why you would never come to England."

"Mom." Danni hesitated. "Rob and I are not in a financial situation that would allow us to do something like that."

"Oh, baby."

"Mom, you know I haven't been able to work. Jack's

heart problem almost wiped us out. Now here I am pregnant again." Danni shrugged. "Things are tough. Our house is too small and old, with no yard or growing room. We're just going through a difficult time."

Now it was Claire's turn to sit back and stare.

"I'm so sorry, Danni. I'm so sorry that I left you."

"Quit saying you're sorry, Mom." Danni put her head in her hands. "Why, Mom? Why didn't you tell me? Why Sarah? You went to Sarah and told her. I just always wondered why."

Claire sighed. "Danni, I knew it had to be Sarah. I couldn't have talked to you about it. We both would have broken down. It was the cowardly thing to do, that's all. I just couldn't face you. But Sarah's so strong."

Claire wept with Danni. There was no more to say about it.

"Tell me about Jack's heart problem. Is he going to be okay?"

Danni nodded. "We think so. The doctors are pleased with his progress. Sarah could probably explain it better. He was born with something called *truncus arteriosus*. It's a heart defect that developed when I was carrying him. I know … um … that it affects the walls in his heart and the aorta and the arteries that pump blood to his lungs.

"He just started having some problems when he was a month old. The doctors said it was congestive heart failure." Danni sighed and continued. "He wasn't growing right, and everything made him get blue looking. The pediatrician heard a heart murmur.

"For some reason, it just didn't get picked up on in the hospital when he was born. Thank God for Sarah. She was with me through everything. His first surgery was when he was six weeks old. They closed the hole in his heart between the two ventricles."

"Oh, Danni." A tear snaked down Claire's face.

"There were more repairs. Jack actually has pieces in his heart from donors like Dad. Of course, he'll have to have more surgeries as he grows because the size of the conduit will need to grow with him. We have to watch him pretty carefully. He's on a lot of pills. I had to learn to check his pulse every day." Danni sighed and shrugged her shoulders. "I just couldn't work, Mom."

"I can't imagine what you went through."

"It wasn't easy. I leaned on Sarah a lot. She took a leave. She was there every step of the way. I don't know what I would have done without her, Mom. I wouldn't have survived. She kept me sane. She took care of all of us."

"I'm glad she was there for you."

"I know she's being really hard on you, Mom, but it's because she had to take over and take care of all of us. She and Matt were great. Just give Sarah some time."

"Time." Claire smiled. "It's what I keep hearing from everyone."

"It's because she's so much like Dad."

"Oh, yes. You'll get no argument from me there."

Claire and Danni finished their meal in silence, just enjoying each other's company. "I've really enjoyed this time together, Danni." Claire smiled.

"Well, we should probably go. It's been so great talking, Mom."

They walked to the car arm in arm, mother and daughter, reconciled.

JOE 2005

RECOLLECTIONS OF THE PAST

Christine took the tie from his hands and chose another from his closet then slipped it around his neck with a little pat. Joe smiled.

"How's your day? I thought we could meet for lunch and check out a couple hotels for the reception."

"I think that could work." Joe reached for a coffee cup. "Coffee?"

"Yes. And juice. What time would be good for you?" she called from the bedroom. "My schedule's tight until about twelve thirty." Christine came into the kitchenette, briefcase in hand, looking sensational in a gray wool suit.

"How 'bout I cab over and pick you up at twelve thirty, then?" Joe leaned over for a kiss. "I'm gonna have such a hot wife."

It was Christine's turn to smile. She smoothed his hair from his forehead and settled at the table with her juice and coffee and the newspaper, their fingers intertwined as they each read a section.

Since they'd moved in together, their lives had taken on a quiet compatibility. Joe had never been happier.

Four or five years back, Joe had felt his life was over. Losing his dad had been a shocking blow, but losing his mom had been monumental.

Joe and his dad had been close but never shared the same connection that Sarah and Dad had. Jack just wasn't around all that much to be the driving force in Joe's life. His mother had been the major influence in his life.

Mom was the one taking him to hockey practice, baseball practice, and swim lessons. Dad decided he should learn to golf when he was about seven. It was one of Joe's fondest memories. No girls around, just him and dad on the course.

Although Jack rarely made it to any of Joe's games during his school years, he always kept a day a week open for golf, weather permitting. They would stay on the course until long after dark, when Jack would protest, "C'mon, Joe; you can't even see your ball!"

"One more hole, Dad," Joe would plead. They were the best of times.

Sometimes Jack would take Joe to the office. Joe thought his dad was larger than life. There were spans as Joe grew up when his dad was distant and seemed to have little time for his children. Joe was unaware that this was when his dad was actively involved in an extramarital affair.

Like his sisters, Joe maintained a hero worship of his father, who, even in his absentia, managed a tight ship.

They all looked to Jack for guidance. Even his mother never made a decision of her own as far back as Joe could remember.

But, like his sisters, he depended on his mother for other things—motherly love, daily care, and that solid reliability that children need. His mom was always there for him. That was why her abandonment was devastating for him even at twenty-one. It came as yet another shocking blow.

And just like Danni, Joe had leaned on Sarah. She had always been the strong one.

"I said, are you daydreaming?"

Joe blinked. "I guess I was. I was thinking about Mom and Dad." He shrugged.

"Joe." Christine leaned close and placed her forehead against his. "She's your mother. You did the right thing to forgive her. I keep thinking how good it would be to have both our entire families at our wedding."

Joe smiled. "Maybe it will happen." He looked at his watch. "If Sarah doesn't chase her away. She's such a hard ass."

Christine frowned. "She really isn't that hard. She tries to come across like that Joe, but she's hurting inside. Maybe worse than you and Danni."

"I don't know. You see things in her that I don't." He stood up. "We need to run."

They parked in the commuters' lot and took separate trains into the city after finalizing their plans to meet up for lunch.

Joe leaned against the seat. *I'm really getting married*, he thought. He'd made plans with Claire to have dinner at their apartment Tuesday, and he was really excited about

having her see their apartment and get to know Christine better.

His cell rang, and he saw Sarah's number come across.

"Hey, baby brother."

"Sarah."

"I know you're on your way to work, and I'm on my way to bed, but I just wanted to get your take on Mom's story."

"I don't know, Sarah. You know, it sounds like things weren't easy for her either."

"C'mon, Joe. You saw the photo. She looked pretty happy."

"I just want to put all the anger behind us."

"Uh, yeah."

"Sarah, Danni told me about the age thing and the grandparent thing, and those are pretty rough things for anyone to go through."

Joe could feel Sarah's icy anger through the phone.

"Hey. C'mon, sis. You're the one with the big heart. You took care of all of us. You can make room for her ... Sarah ... answer me. I'm gonna hang up, but I love you."

"Love you too. I think."

Joe smiled.

"Talk to you soon."

"Unbelievable." Sarah rang off. Was she the only one who felt this way?

MATTHEW 2005

THOUGHTS OF WISDOM

Matt kept his word and left the office at noon on Monday. Claire was waiting for him, holding a shoebox.

"I think I have everything we need."

Together, they went to the insurance agent and insured the Buick. Then they went to the secretary of state's office, and Claire renewed her license.

From there, they visited two banks and a credit union. Claire was shocked at the amount of money she had. They left the credit union, and Claire held a hand against her stomach.

"You okay, Claire?" Matt asked, concerned.

"Matthew, I'm a rich woman."

"Well then, I'll let you buy lunch."

"I'm serious!"

"So am I."

They sat in a diner together. Matt ordered iced tea and a sandwich; Claire, a salad and coffee. With her fork she played with the unappetizing brown salad.

"Matthew, I want to pay you kids back. And Joe, I want to pay for his college loans."

Matt chewed his sandwich thoughtfully. "Well, what do you plan to do, Claire?"

"What do you mean?"

"I mean, what are your plans?"

"Well," Claire answered thoughtfully, "I plan to go home to England sometime soon. I have a new life there. But I also plan to return for the birth of Danni's baby, and I intend to visit all my grandchildren on a regular basis. I intend to never disappear again."

Matt shrugged. "Well, Claire. If you want to pay Joe back, that's fine. And if you want to put money in Abbie and Aimee's college fund, that's okay. But Joe and Christine are fine. And the girls are fine. The only ones not fine in this family are Danni and Rob. They're hurting."

Claire sipped her coffee thoughtfully. Matt leaned forward over the table. "Claire," he said, "think about this: Danni and Rob could use your house. It would suit their family much better and still be someplace to stay when you come home. They'd be moving to a better school district."

Claire's eyes glistened. "Oh, Matthew." She grasped his hand. "That's a wonderful idea. What better use for our home? I don't need the house."

"It's something to think about anyway. And the money thing, I'm not sure how rich you think you are, but you're basically a young woman. You don't earn a lot of money at

the bookstore I'm assuming," he added. "You want to travel back and forth; that's not going to be cheap. Maybe you should think about holding on to some of that money."

"Matthew, it's a lot of money. I can share and still be okay. I guess it's a little like buying love, but I don't care."

"Just take some time before you do anything. Jack must have had a financial advisor, an accountant or attorney. I know there was a will."

"Yes, Paul Beckett. I met him after Jack died. But I was in a fog then. Do you think I should make an appointment?"

"I think it might be a good idea."

Claire sipped her coffee thoughtfully.

"Claire, there's something else." Matt seemed unsure where to start. "While you were gone ... well, after a few years, three exactly, we just weren't sure if something might have happened to you. We were afraid; Sarah was afraid, that you might not be alive." Matt looked into Claire's eyes. "We hired a private detective." Matt pulled the well-worn grainy photo from his pocket. "I'm sorry."

Claire, shocked, stared at her smiling face, arm in arm with David. They were loaded down with packages. She chewed her thumbnail.

"Sarah carried it around for months. I finally made her put it away."

"What must she think?"

"Well, none of us knew what you had gone through. His report just said that you were doing fine living and working in England. We only hired him to find you."

"No wonder she hates me."

"She doesn't hate you, Claire."

She shook her head and wiped a tear away with her napkin.

They finished their lunch in silence.

Matt checked his watch. "It's three forty-five. Sarah will be looking for me soon."

Claire paid the bill, as promised. They drove in quiet for a time.

"I need to go next door and see Mrs. Bloom. You know, your Sarah was named after her. And Danni was named after Daniel."

Matt's eyebrows went up. "No kidding."

"They were my saviors on many occasions. I don't think I would have survived the early years of my marriage without Sarah."

"Things were tough with Jack?"

Claire shrugged. "I won't talk bad about him. I loved him. We just had some difficult times."

"You're a piece of work, Claire." Matt chuckled softly. "The way I remember Jack; well, it was mostly about him."

"He was a good father. The kids adored him."

"Yeah. I'm married to Sarah. Remember?"

Claire sat quietly.

"Sarah said he was gone a lot for work when she was growing up."

Claire just stared out the window.

"Okay, I get it. You don't want to talk about it. We'll just drop it."

Matt concentrated on driving.

"He was unfaithful." Claire's voice broke. "It wasn't just one. There were many others."

Matt reached across the front seat and squeezed Claire's hand. He couldn't find any words to say. They rode together in quiet until Matt pulled in the drive.

"I'm sorry I asked, Claire."

"Please don't say anything to Sarah."

"I won't."

"Matthew, I don't know what I ever did to deserve such a wonderful son-in-law."

"Please say that to Sarah."

Claire laughed. "I can't thank you enough. I feel like I did the first time I got my driver's license. I can't wait to drive the Buick!"

"Rob has kept it in great shape."

Matt headed home, and Claire settled down in the kitchen with tea. Talking about Jack had brought back more memories. She cradled her head in her hands. She tried so hard to think of the good instead of the bad. She decided it was time to pay a visit to the Blooms to take her mind off Jack.

JACK 1982

BLAME AND DENIAL

Jack was restless. He'd been good for so long. The breakup with Donna had almost destroyed his marriage, even more so than the affair itself.

Claire had learned to be tolerant of his affairs and needs but had been intolerant of his grief and remorse over the loss of Donna.

Jack yearned for that extra emotional attachment he'd experienced with Donna. There was Teri, of course. Teri was convenient and willing on occasion, but like Jack, she was married and unwilling to risk her marriage. Thus, Jack lacked the control component in the relationship that his psyche desperately needed.

Donna had dangled the carrot of control during their affair, never quite becoming submissive.

Jack was in a constant state of obsession and lust, fighting for control. No matter how close they became, Jack felt Donna always held something back.

After seven long years, part of him still grieved for Donna. He'd had several wonderful years with Claire. She would always own his heart, and since they'd reconciled, they had rekindled their relationship of years past. Jack's world was Claire and the children.

Joseph was two years old, a handful. Claire seemed always tired. Jack was spending a lot of time at the golf course. He'd heard a lot of talk in the locker room about the new beer cart girl, but he had yet to see her.

Colleen was everything that Jack had never been attracted to. She had fiery red hair that she wore in a thick braid down her back. She was full-figured with large, heavy breasts and creamy white skin that burned and freckled easily, giving her a young look. She had an overbite when she smiled and a dimpled chin.

Her personality suited Jack. She was receptive to his flirting, eager for attention. His offhanded compliments made her glow, and she didn't rebuff his advancements when he let his hand rest on her thigh.

He asked her out several times. She declined. Jack's conscience was bothering him. The girls had been weighing heavily on his mind, but he was conflicted. He loved Claire; he sometimes just needed more.

Opportunity presented itself one early evening when a sudden thunderstorm came up. Jack was finishing up the back nine and drove his cart toward the clubhouse. Lightning flashed around him. He watched as Colleen parked the beer cart behind the garage, unlocked the door, and made a dash inside, and he changed direction and followed her into the garage.

She turned, startled.

"Sorry." He smiled. "I just grabbed the first shelter." He shook the water from himself.

"I don't think you're supposed to be in here."

Jack crooked his thumb toward the door. "Hey! Do you want a guy to get struck by lightning out there?" He grinned. "I'm not going to touch any of your equipment. Okay?"

Colleen looked hesitant. "I guess." She wrapped her arms around herself and shivered nervously. "I just don't want to get in any trouble, that's all."

"Now, Colleen. I think you're the prettiest thing this golf course has had around here in a long time. Do you think I'd do anything to get you in trouble?"

She smiled. "No."

"I have a warm windbreaker in my bag here." He kept talking, rummaging through his golf bag. "You're shivering. Let me wrap you up in this."

Jack put the jacket around her, letting his hands rub up and down her arms. Colleen trembled. He leaned in toward her. "Why won't you go out with me?" he asked her.

Colleen breathed in and out softly. "You're married, Mr. Bradley."

"Jack," he whispered, grazing her cheek with his lips. "Call me Jack. I'm separated. It's difficult. We try to make the best of things for the children's sake. But we live our own lives."

"You're older."

Jack looked surprised. "How old are you?" he asked her.

"Twenty."

Jack continued to let his hand slide up and down her arm. "You're a woman, Colleen, and I'm a man. Do you really believe that age is relevant?"

212

She shrugged and shook her head no. "I had a boyfriend. We broke up last year."

"Well, you know how hard separations are, don't you? I know I'm attracted to you. And I think you're attracted to me. And we wouldn't be hurting anyone if we got together."

She looked up at him and let her arms fall down to her sides, inviting him closer. Jack pulled her to him and began kissing her neck, her mouth. He fondled and caressed her and backed her up to a desk.

"Not here." She pushed him back breathlessly. "I can't. We haven't even had a date or anything. I'm not that kind of girl."

Jack clenched his jaw and gave her a tight smile. "You want flowers and candy. I can do that. But I want more. You're not in high school anymore. It's you I want. So if you're not that kind of girl, I need to know before I walk out that door." He pointed to the lightening sky.

Colleen hesitated and bit her lip. "I can go out on Friday."

Jack smiled. "How about if we order in at your place? I'll bring the flowers and candy."

"I live with my parents."

Jack's face clouded. This was a dilemma. Jack's extras always worked with him or had their own place. He couldn't risk taking her to his office after hours. And he worried about publicly flaunting an affair by renting rooms. It meant they would have to drive far away from town. He couldn't risk running into someone he knew. That would make lying to Claire even more difficult.

Jack sighed. Colleen looked at him hopefully. He stared at the wet shirt clinging to her chest. She might be worth the risk.

CLAIRE 2005

THE VISIT

Mrs. Bloom must have had a premonition. She had decided to bake an afternoon coffee cake and was cooling it on the counter when the doorbell rang.

"Mrs. Bloom." Claire stood in the doorway, smiling.

Sarah Bloom moved surprisingly spry for her age when she grabbed Claire and pulled her into a great bear hug. "Oh, child. Look at you."

Both women cried. They settled at Mrs. Bloom's familiar Formica kitchen table; unchanged after thirty-six years. Claire wolfed down a large wedge of coffee cake.

"I'd forgotten how wonderful your cooking is."

They talked for two hours straight. Claire insisted that Mrs. Bloom do the updating first, as she wanted to hear all about her life. "Tell me about Daniel and Samuel."

Mrs. Bloom, in turn, listened with compassion as Claire recited her story.

"I was hoping you were here to stay."

"Well, that is one of the things I wanted to talk to you about. How would you feel about living next door to Danni and Rob and the children?"

"Daniel's namesake? Why that's a wonderful thought, Claire. To have children as neighbors again. To see that old swing set and tree house used; now that would be a good thing."

Claire smiled. "I agree. I'm having the house transferred to Danni's name. They've been having a difficult time financially. Little Jack has been sick a lot."

"I know. Poor thing." Mrs. Bloom clucked. "We always inquire about the little tyke. Roberto comes pretty frequently to check out the house and car. He's always so friendly and helpful to Daniel whenever we need work on our vehicles or the house. He always comes for coffee and pie. He's a fine young man." Sarah Bloom nodded. "Yes, having Danni and Roberto here would make my Daniel happy."

"And I'll have a place to stay when I come for a visit."

"Speaking of visits, your Sarah spent some time with me some weeks back. She was full of questions; had been sorting around through papers and photos and such. I hope I didn't say anything untoward."

Claire patted the old woman's hands. "There are no untoward words that come from you. Only words of comfort and grace."

The two women embraced and said their good-byes.

"It's like we'll be neighbors again."

Claire hesitated at the door. "Sarah, I never thanked you properly for always being there for me."

"Shush now. Shush. You gave us much joy in return."

Claire walked that familiar path between the two homes. Some stars were twinkling on the horizon. She would wait and take the Buick out tomorrow. She was tired and felt that she could sleep now.

SARAH

THE PHONE CALL

Sarah and the girls had just returned from ballet. Matt wasn't home yet but would be soon, and Sarah had steaks defrosting for supper.

She had just sent the girls off to do homework and was headed into the kitchen when the phone rang.

"Sarah?"

"Yes?"

"This is Iris Neville. Dr. Iris Neville. I'm calling from London. I'm a friend of your mother's."

Sarah's face clouded. She was instantly wary. "I know who you are, Dr. Neville."

"Good. I mean, I'm glad I don't have to explain myself. I'm relieved you know who I am because I'm worried about your mother, Sarah. I spoke with her yesterday. She sounds on edge. Goodness, listen to me. I'm babbling."

"Did she ask you to call me?"

"No. Heavens, no. I'd prefer she not know that I rang you up."

Sarah became angry. "Well, why would you call me? I am not my mother's guardian. She hasn't been a part of my life for—oh, let's see—almost five years."

"Sarah, please. I just thought you needed to know what your mother went through."

"Oh, we've all heard the story. Well, you should hear our story, Dr. Neville. The story of the family she turned her back on."

"Sarah, you're a nurse. Surely you are knowledgeable about mental illness. How can you lack compassion for your mother?"

"My mother's problems were self-generated."

"I'm speechless." Iris paused. "Do you know about role-modeling Sarah? Your father had a fashioning effect on your mother. It was easy to exert control on a person as young as your mother was, especially when there were no external influences."

"How dare you lecture me about my father." Sarah bristled.

"Too much anxiety can lower one's ability to make sound judgments. Your mother was subjected to extreme emotional abuse, which, in turn, caused her extreme anxiety."

"Mrs. Neville, er...Dr. Neville. I would think it unethical for you to discuss my mother's case with me."

"Sarah, surely you know that I'm calling as your mother's friend. I'm worried about her wellbeing. I am trying to make you understand. Your mother was a person with a strongly externalized locus of control. She was so used to conforming for your father and living under his

control that she was unable to function on her own. Are you aware that she was depressive and suicidal on many occasions?"

"Most of my memories are associated with my father."

"Your mother just couldn't handle the pressure to carry on her role as mother. She lost all hope."

Sarah chuckled. "It's all so dramatic."

"Sarah, she ran away when she became dissociative. She fell into psychological disorganization and inactivity. She lost all memory of her family, Sarah."

"We all lost hope, Dr. Neville. We all worried and cried and prayed and felt guilty for whatever we might have done to drive her away. But we never forgot who she was!"

"Your mother's death would certainly have followed had we not intervened, and it wouldn't have taken another suicide attempt, Sarah. She endured electroconvulsive therapy sessions, drug therapy, and psychoanalysis. It was a long and difficult road back."

"Well, I can't forgive her sins against the family."

"There are many shades of sin, Sarah. Your mother was sick, not bad. Her heart is not black. She was simply lost. If she's sinned at all, it is pale in comparison to what you hold her to."

"She is still lost to me, Dr. Neville. I have to go. My children are waiting."

Iris held the silent phone in her hand.

MATTHEW

SO HEAVY MY HEART

They all sat down to dinner for grilled steaks, and Matt talked about his afternoon with Claire. The girls were chatty and excited.

"Now Grandma can take us shopping!" Abbie said.

Sarah was glum. Matt silently worried about her. Since Claire had returned, Sarah had become this angry, volatile stranger. He wanted his wife back. Matt wondered if he should share their discussion of turning the house over to Danni and Rob, if it would cheer up her mood; then he thought better of it. He would wait and let Claire make that announcement.

He reached over and squeezed her hand resting on the table. "Good dinner, babe."

She gave him a brief smile then turned toward the girls. "Abbie, did you get all your homework done?"

"Yes."

"Well, you bring it down after dinner, and I'll check it," said Matt. "Let's all get the kitchen done so we have some time before bed."

Sarah and the girls worked in the kitchen while Matt cleaned the grill and pushed it back in the garage. Then Sarah had the girls put a load of laundry in and listened to them grouse. She expected the girls to know how to handle housework and laundry. It was just too much for one person to work full time and keep up the house.

She leaned against the counter and yawned. In a few hours, she'd be leaving for work.

Matt checked Abbie's homework while Sarah and Aimee read; then Matt horse-played with them both for a while until Sarah shooed them off to bed.

Abbie, sullen and angry, argued with her. "We're having fun with Daddy!"

Sarah was reminded of herself as a little girl, so angry with her mother for denying her additional time with her dad, sending her off to bed when Dad was just getting home or not getting home at all. She was so conflicted with feelings. If she left things up to Matt, he would never look at the clock.

"Brush your teeth and wash your face. We'll be up in a few minutes to tuck you in."

Sarah puttered around in the shower and the bathroom, getting ready for work.

Matt tried to start a conversation, but Sarah was distant.

She pondered telling him about the phone call but instead decided not to share for fear he would take her mother's side. She didn't want to fight again.

Matt, unaware of Sarah's dilemma, felt helpless in the wake of her brooding disposition. He walked her to her car, wondering what to say. "Be careful" was all that came out.

Matt stood in the drive, feeling far too inadequate to handle the situation with Sarah and her mother. But it was most certainly affecting all of them. He sighed then walked into the house with a heavy heart.

SARAH

DOUBTS

Sarah's heart was heavy also. She too wanted things to be the way they were. She just couldn't cave on this one.

The phone call from Mom's friend had rattled her. Sarah knew she'd come across as bitter, unforgiving, and angry. Because she was.

She had walled her heart off from her mother, and Sarah wondered why the others could forgive and forget so easily.

Certainly, Sarah hadn't been as close to her mother as Danni and Joe had. She wasn't really sure why. She'd just always preferred her dad.

And she couldn't help but wonder what might have happened if she had been more tuned in to her dad's health. She was angry that her mother hadn't talked with

her about Dad's headaches. She'd only heard about them from Danni at the funeral home.

In the years that followed Mom's disappearance, the headaches had grown in importance to Sarah. She even believed that had she been informed, she could have insisted that Dad get checked out. Maybe even the stroke could have been averted altogether.

Sarah's jaw was clenched and becoming sore. She recalled arguing with her mother when Dad worked late or didn't come home. Mom always had an answer. She remembered catching a whiff of something on Dad's collar that wasn't Mom's Tabu. She recalled being confused and conflicted. Dad would never have fooled around on Mom.

Why was she even thinking about this? Sarah was angry with herself. *What is wrong with me?*

She shook her head, sighed, and pulled into the parking ramp. *A hard night at work is just what I need*, she thought.

JACK 1982

SO ENDS ANOTHER

The affair with Colleen lasted almost six months, but Jack quickly tired of her immaturity and her neediness. Once, at the golf course, she had driven up to his foursome and behaved inappropriately. Jack's coworkers were uncomfortable.

Jack was enraged and confronted her that night at their motel. "Don't you ever get familiar with me in public again!"

Colleen sat on the edge of the bed sniveling, tissue in hand. "But—"

"Do you have any idea that I have a reputation in this town?"

"But what about us? I thought you were separated." She sobbed. "I love you, Jack. It's just not fair we can't tell everyone we're in love."

Jack stared at her, incredulous. "Don't make something out of this it's not," he said threateningly. "I won't ever leave my wife. You know why I'm here, Colleen."

Colleen placed her head in her hands and wept. "I'm not that kind of girl," she spoke softly.

"Don't kid yourself. Now take your jeans off. And leave your top on." Jack started unzipping his pants.

"I won't," she cried. "I won't."

"Colleen." Jack reached out and smoothed her hair back. "It's okay. You don't have to do anything. I'm just upset because I don't want you to get the wrong idea, that's all. Remember, I said we could do this without hurting anybody."

Jack sat on the bed next to her and wrapped an arm around her shaking shoulders. "I didn't mean to make you cry. I care about you; you know that."

"No." She wept, refusing to look up at him. "You don't."

Jack grasped her wrist and guided her hand to himself. "Do you feel how much I care about you?" he whispered against her ear.

"Oh, Jack," she sobbed.

Jack laid her back against the bed and helped her with her jeans.

Driving home later, Jack worried how he was going to unleash himself from Colleen. And Colleen, desperate and afraid, wondered how to keep Jack from tiring of her.

In the end, he just stopped calling her. Colleen made several halfhearted attempts to speak with him on the course, but his withering looks made her shy away.

Eventually, Colleen quit her job and moved on. Jack

was filled with regret for his actions—regret that, for some reason he couldn't define, he needed more. More than Claire could provide.

Jack was the envy of his friends whenever he had Claire on his arm. Yet as attractive and beautiful as she was, she just wasn't enough. He blamed her for some vague inadequacies that made him seek comfort elsewhere. Whenever Jack rationalized his infidelities, it always came down to Claire's faults. She was the cause for their troubles.

JOE 2005

A WISH FULFILLED

The doorbell sounded at Joe and Christine's. "She's here, Joe," Christine called, wiping her hands on a towel and heading to the door.

"Welcome." She smiled, pulled Claire inside, and embraced her warmly. "Joe's in the bathroom." Christine rolled her eyes.

Claire chuckled, looked around the apartment. "It's gorgeous, Christine!" Claire meant it. She walked around touching and admiring their artwork and antiques.

"Mom!" Joe emerged from the bathroom, newspaper in hand.

"The apple doesn't fall far from the tree, I see." Claire laughed and gave Joe a hug. "I was admiring your place."

Joe looked proud. "Christine has taught me a lot. She has great taste."

"I can see that."

228

Christine brought in a tray of wine, cheeses, and fruit.

Claire was at ease and comfortable with the two of them. It was good to relax and laugh.

Christine had cooked a lovely dinner. She and Joe were full of questions about London. Claire, happy to talk about the place she now considered home, was animated and informative.

"We'll definitely be visiting," Joe said.

"I can't wait to antique shop," said Christine.

"Oh, there are so many great places."

Claire shared Matt's idea of turning the house over to Danni and Rob. Both of them thought it was a great idea. Joe told Claire that he and Christine had been looking at ways for Danni to do some contract work from home, which would help them out. Claire was pleased.

She brought up the idea of repayment, which was shrugged off by both of them.

"The loans are paid, Mom. Christine and I have good incomes. Help Danni, and save your money to come back for visits."

The hours passed swiftly. Joe yawned.

"Oh my." Claire looked amazed that so much time had passed. "I've kept you kids up far too late."

"No." Christine patted her head. "He's always yawning after dinner."

They laughed. Then they made plans to get together again soon.

"When are you going back, Mom?"

Claire paused. "I want to try again with Sarah. I'm not ready to give up."

"I'm glad," Christine told her. "She's not as hard as she comes across. I think she's just hurting."

"I've caused that hurt."

"Mom, you need to let it go. Maybe the one you need forgiveness from the most is yourself."

Claire smiled weakly and embraced both of them. "You're probably right. Thank you both."

When the evening ended, Claire felt better than she had. Perhaps she would go see Sarah tomorrow.

THE CONFRONTATION

Matt had taken the girls to Abbie's soccer practice, giving Sarah the time to get some housework done. She looked outside at the darkening sky. Thinking that practice might get cancelled, she wondered about starting dinner early since it definitely looked like rain.

Coffee cup in hand, Sarah carried a load of folded towels upstairs. She stripped the girls' beds and was putting on clean sheets when she heard the doorbell ring.

Sarah walked to the window and saw the Buick in the drive. She sighed, trudged downstairs, and let her mom in.

"If you're looking for Matt or the girls, they're not here."

"Actually, Sarah, I was looking for you. I am going to the cemetery to sit by your father. I was hoping you would come along. We could talk."

"Mom, I have a lot of things to do."

"Please. Can't you spare just a few minutes to talk to me?" Claire pleaded.

"Would you like coffee?"

"Yes, thanks. Can we sit down?"

Claire sat at the table while Sarah poured another coffee for her mom then wondered where she'd left hers.

"Still black, or has that changed too?"

"No." Claire smiled. "Still black."

They settled at the table. Claire prayed she'd find the right words.

"Sarah, I meant it when I said I'm sorry."

"Good." Sarah sounded matter-of-fact.

"I plan on staying in England. It's my home now. But I will never desert you again, Sarah."

Claire leaned toward her daughter, who stiffened and retreated from her mother's nearness.

"You have my word. I'll never hurt any of my family again."

Sarah stood up and backed up against the sink. "You know, Mom, I have so much to do—"

"Sarah, look at me. I'm here. It's like you can't even see me."

"You're nothing more than a shadow to me of what you used to be. I don't have faith in shadows."

"I'm out of the shadows. I'm here now."

Sarah shook her head back and forth. "No."

"I need your forgiveness, Sarah, please."

"Okay. You want to be forgiven? You're forgiven. Now, can I go about my business and you go about yours? I really don't care to be around you." Sarah's anger was raw. "Why can't you understand that?" She walked purposefully toward the hall, Claire on her heels.

"Please, Sarah, I need to hear you say the words from your heart." Claire reached out to turn her daughter toward her.

Sarah reacted. In a rage, she pushed her mother backward. Claire slammed into the wall against a painting, knocking it to the floor. Claire slid down in the shards of broken glass, stunned.

Sarah was also stunned—stunned that she could have reacted so violently. Claire was broken. She rolled limply over on her knees in the shards of glass.

Sarah, frozen, stared down at her mother. "I'm sorry," she whispered. She bent over Claire. "I didn't mean to." She reached down to help her up.

Claire shrugged her off and stood slowly. She shouldered past Sarah and walked toward the door.

Sarah was angry that her mother had pushed her over the edge. She stood rigidly, back against the wall, her fists clenched tightly.

"You'll never hear those words from my heart, Mother," she whispered through clenched teeth. "My heart is closed to you."

Claire didn't turn around. She opened the door and walked woodenly to her car, fumbled with the lock, and collapsed behind the wheel, her soul in anguish.

She was unaware of her bleeding hands and knees. Only that she had failed someone she loved once again.

REGRETS

Matt and the girls piled in the front door, wet and laughing. Matt took one look at Sarah crumpled among the broken glass and ran to her. She was pale and shaking, and her finger was bleeding.

"I was trying to clean it up," she spoke between hiccupping sobs.

"What happened?" He knelt down and lifted her up in his big arms, looking over her finger.

"I don't know." She shook her head back and forth. "I don't really know." She laid her head on his shoulder as he carried her to the bathroom. The girls were on his heels.

"I'm going to be sick. Matt, put me down." Sarah fell to her knees in front of the toilet, her stomach lurching, but nothing came up. "I'm sorry. I'm sorry."

Matt stared at her, concerned. "Sarah, did you knock the picture down?"

"It happened so fast. She came here, and I asked her to leave…"

"Who came, Sarah?" Matt looked at her hard. "Who came? Your mom?"

"She wanted to put her arms around me. I shoved her backward. I pushed her hard. I think I hurt her."

"Sarah," Matt said softly, shocked. Abigail and Aimee stood in the bathroom door horrified.

"You pushed Grandma?" Abbie screamed.

"Abigail! You and your sister go to your room now!" Matt said with authority.

"How could you hurt Grandma?" Abbie stood her ground.

Matt pointed upstairs. "I said go, now."

Aimee ran for the stairs, crying, and Abbie stomped up them loudly, chastising her mother. "She just wants to be with us, that's all!"

Matt sat Sarah on the stool while he examined her finger, washed it, and bandaged it.

Sarah wiped at the tears streaming down her face. "I've really done it this time, haven't I?" she whispered.

"How bad is she hurt?"

"I don't know. I know she limped to the car."

"But she was able to drive away?"

"Yes. I don't know what happened to me, Matt." Sarah shook her head. "I can't imagine myself ever doing anything so awful. How did I get so angry?"

"You've always been hotheaded."

"No, not like that."

Matt shrugged. "Well, I need to go find her."

"No." Sarah stood up. "I need to go find her."

"No way. You stay with the girls. There's been enough violence today."

Sarah grabbed his arm. "No, Matt." She glared at him.

235

"I need to make this right. I can't let this go. I have to talk to her myself. I'm the one she needs right now."

"If she sees you coming, she'll probably run."

"I have to do this, Matt."

He hesitated and then put his jacket down. "Sarah, your anger, the bitterness—it's affecting us all." Matt looked away and sighed.

"I know." Sarah wrapped her arms around him.

"Okay. You go. But if you need a mediator, you call me. Understand?"

Sarah nodded.

"Do you have any idea where she might go?"

"I know exactly where she was going. She was going to the cemetery to see Dad. I'll find her."

Matt walked her to the car.

"I'm so sorry, Matt."

"Your mom needs to hear that."

"Tell the girls that I love them. That I'm sorry."

"Do you have your cell phone?"

"Yes."

"Well, call." He stood in the drive, hands in his pockets as she drove away.

Sarah headed to Collingwood Memorial.

RECONCILIATION

The cemetery was deserted. Claire's mind was blank when she entered. She had absolutely no memory of the graveside service or where Jack was buried. She only knew it was Collingwood Memorial from the death certificate she had carried to the bank.

The office was open, and Claire walked in. A gray-haired man sat at a desk and stared with alarm at Claire's bloody legs and hands.

"Need some help?" he asked her.

Claire realized how she must look. "Oh, I'm fine really. A little accident in my garage. I'm looking for a grave. Jack Marlon Bradley."

The man gave Claire the once over then shuffled to the file cabinet. "Bradley, Jack Marlon. He's in Section W-8. If you look on this map here, I can show you."

Claire got her directions and climbed back into the Buick. She wound through the cemetery and found the grave without too much trouble. She sat down on the

grass beside the headstone, unmindful of her coat. She was a mess now anyway.

Being there beside Jack brought back a flood of memories. *Have I really been back in the States such a short time? And gone away from my children so long that ties are broken forever?*

Claire had relied so heavily on Sarah's acceptance because she was the anchor of the family, just as Jack had been. Even if she could maintain a positive relationship with Danni and Joe, what would it do to their relationship with Sarah? Would it be fair to them? Would she ultimately be destroying the integrity of what was left of their family? Would her occasional visits cause more harm than joy? And if she wasn't allowed to see Abbie and Aimee, how would that affect their relationship with their cousins?

No. Without Sarah, she would be forced to break close ties with all of them. That was the cause of her anguish. Once again she had hurt the ones she loved most.

Claire, on her knees, let tears fall upon Jack's grave. "Oh, Jack," she cried out. "I'm not up to this battle. I'm sorry, Jack. I've disappointed everyone yet another time."

Claire's grief was palpable. Every fiber in her being ached. She was unable to control the release of emotions that had been hidden away for so long. "I loved you, Jack. I loved you."

"Mother."

Claire started at Sarah's voice behind her.

"Go away," she whispered without turning around.

"Mother, I'm sorry."

"Go away, Sarah." Claire stifled a sob. "Please, just go away. I don't want to fight anymore."

"I didn't come to fight."

Claire raised an arm behind her and waved Sarah away. "You were right," she said. "I had no right to come back. Please, Sarah. Just leave me alone."

Tears streamed down Sarah's face. She knelt behind her mother and tenderly placed a hand on her shoulder.

"Mom." Sarah's voice choked with emotion. "Please. I'm here to ask for your forgiveness. I don't want to be angry anymore. I want my mother back. Please, Mom. Talk to me. It's all I've ever wanted. I know I've been wrong."

The words spilled forth from Sarah like a catharsis of her own. "Forgive me, Mom. I want Abbie and Aimee to have their grandmother. I need you back in my life." She sobbed.

"Sarah." Claire turned and placed a hand alongside her cheek. "Sarah." She looked into her daughter's eyes, Jack's eyes. "I'm the one who needs forgiveness."

Sarah fell into her mother's arms, melting into her strong embrace. It had been so long. She felt the grip of anger loosen from her heart, and she was filled with peace. Her prayers had been answered.

Sarah, overcome, was unable to speak. They stayed on their knees, locked in an embrace neither one wanted to break. "We need to talk, Mom," she said. "And I'm ready to listen."

The cold, misting rain crept beneath their collars. Sarah lifted her head. "You're cold, Mom. Let's get out of the rain."

"We do have a lot to talk about." Claire looked into her eyes. "I'm leaving for England soon, Sarah."

"No." Sarah pulled away. Her face clouded over. "We're just making up. You can't turn around and say you're leaving again. You can't."

Claire shrugged. "I would extend for a while." She smiled. "Now that I have a reason, but I have a home now in England. I'm in love again, Sarah. It's a different kind of love than your father. But I love him, and I want to make a life with him. Your Matthew helped me make some sound decisions, and I have plans for another trip home soon. Sarah, I plan never to be apart for long again."

"I just feel like if you leave, you'll never come back."

"Sarah, I want you and Danni and Joe to meet David. I want him to meet my grandchildren. I came back to reconcile with all of you; to be a part of your lives again."

Claire grasped both of Sarah's hands in her own. "Don't you see why I needed your forgiveness? I've gone through my whole life feeling I had nothing of value to give; that I was nothing. All of that therapy I went through means nothing unless I am redeemed by my family. And you are the anchor of this family, Sarah."

Claire sighed. "What I put all of you through. I've had to live with my sins, Sarah. It's a terrible burden."

"Don't you know, Mom? There are many shades of sin."

Claire stared at her daughter, Jack's child, so like him in looks and personality. They walked hand in hand to their cars.

"There's a coffee shop on the corner. Let's go there." Sarah pointed in the direction.

They sat together in a booth, knees touching, their hands cradling steaming cups of tea. They talked for an hour, each pouring feelings out that had been pent up for so long. Sarah listened as Claire spoke of her youth, the indiscretion that caused Sarah to be born, the struggles of her marriage as a child bride and mother.

Sarah spoke freely, and apologies for so many wrongs were laid on the table.

Sarah talked about her demons of anger and bitterness and her need for control; Claire, of her inadequacies, her desperate need for love and approval.

They spoke of separation, of needs unmet, of distance, and of duty to family

Sarah talked about the anger that had held her heart for so long.

It was difficult to talk about marriage, but Sarah was ready to listen. Claire spoke of infidelity, the heartache that had gripped her soul for so long. She told Sarah of her deep love and loyalty to Jack, shared her sorrow when she broke the connections to her family, the thing she cherished the most and lost.

Then she shared her plans to turn the house over to Danni and Rob. It made Sarah smile.

It was dark when they left the coffee shop. Claire left the waitress a ten-dollar tip for taking up her booth for so long and leaving them alone.

They drove to Sarah and Matt's to share their happiness with Matt and the girls.

They both would need more time to heal, but Sarah felt a release for the first time in many years.

Claire knew there would be much more work ahead; bridges to build with her children. But she finally felt up to the task. For Claire's soul was redeemed, and life had given her a second chance.